T0279251

THANKS FOR LISTENING

ALSO BY MOLLY HORAN

Epically Earnest

THANKS FOR LISTENING

MOLLY HORAN

HARPER

An Imprint of HarperCollinsPublishers

Thanks for Listening

Library of Congress Control Number: 2023948736
ISBN 978-0-06-331842-7

Typography by Samira Iravani
24 25 26 27 28 LBC 5 4 3 2 1
First Edition

To Sam

I went to Reddit for book dedication advice.

Not sure it helped, but you do. Love you.

ONE

There is currently a flyer for the drama club Halloween bake sale stapled to my best friend's forearm because no one ever, ever listens to me.

"Get it out," Essie howls, as three freshmen techies seem to consider her plea.

"No one is getting it out besides a medical professional at urgent care," I say, squeezing her hand as I look closer at my friend's former arm/current community notice board.

"Essie!" Talley's voice rips through the entire backstage, and I barely have time to figure out how word of Essie's injury could have possibly, humanly, even with the combined speed of texts and drama gossip, reached him on the other side of school in the band room, before he's grabbing Essie's other hand.

"I thought it was unplugged. I just wanted to see how heavy it was," Essie sobs, as Talley nods like this is a completely normal explanation rather than two things that could have been fact-checked with a combination of Google and just looking. Or, you know, listening to her best friend and stage manager when I said actors should under no circumstances handle the power tools.

"Do you think we should just yank it out?" Talley asks me, peering at the now blood-splattered sketch of a cupcake dangling from his girl-friend's arm.

"No. We're waiting for Greg to get his car, and then we're driving her to urgent care, where we will explain to someone who went to medical school that our future valedictorian was playing with a staple gun, and we're hoping the only memento of the occasion will be this flyer and not nerve damage." I put my hands on my hips, in what I hope is an effective power stance. I also adjust my headset, which is absolutely not necessary to wear during a set build day, but makes me feel like I have at least some semblance of authority, even if my friends keep proving me wrong.

"My mom is going to give me so much shit if it's not covered," Essie starts.

"I'll google it—give me the name of her insurance." I pull out my phone.

Mallory, a junior in charge of props, pipes up. "I think, since it's a staple gun, the metal bits don't really hook under."

"That is possible, even probable, but when any kind of metal thing pierces your body, the rule is do not take it out unless you are a medical professional. And these are industrial-strength staples," I say, wishing this was a rule I was bringing up with my crew for the first time instead of one of the numbered rules I sent out with the drama club welcome email at the start of the school year.

"I'm just gonna do it," Essie says, at least giving me enough warning so I was looking up from my phone as she pulled the staple out of her skin.

She looks triumphant for a moment, haughty even, ready to explain how wrong I was since we weren't showered in her blood. But when she looks down at the (granted) modest trickle, she passes out so fast, not even Talley can catch her. I know without looking that she has landed on the dropped staple.

"Do you think we should call Mr. L?" Mallory asks, as Talley kneels by Essie's head to try to wake her up. I just nod. Apparently after there have been at least two medical emergencies, someone is willing to take my advice.

TWO

"I'm home," I call as I walk through our front door, dropping my backpack and two tote bags onto a pile that already includes Brian's lacrosse stuff and Dad's gym bag. I know the mess drives Mom crazy, but I personally like our little bag sculpture. It's like our collective family art project. I pull off my frog beanie (the one with frogs embroidered around the edges, not the one that actually looks like a frog head, which I also own) and place it on top, so it has a hat now too. I may not be an artist like Talley and Essie, but that doesn't mean I can't add artistic flourishes in my day-to-day life.

"You doing Shakespeare?" Brian asks, as he comes crashing down the stairs, making the family pictures on the wall shake. He's wearing a T-shirt that reads "John Adams High School Lacrosse Forever," and I'm not sure whether it's meant to imply he's part of an unending line of guys hitting each other with sticks across the decades, or just an indication the coaches aren't emotionally preparing them for a post–high school reality.

"No, we're doing *A Christmas Carol*. Same as always," I say, kicking my shoes off.

"Cool." He looks me over. "So, you're going full horror this year? Like the ghosts are gonna, like, freak Scrooge out by pulling off their heads and stuff?"

"What are you talking about? We invite the elementary schools every year—we're not staging *Saw*."

"Oh. I just thought 'cause of the blood," he says, motioning to my hoodie, which does have some blood stains across the chest.

"Right. Backstage accident."

"Did one of those lights fall on someone?"

"If one of the lights fell on someone, they'd be dead. I wouldn't be so chill if I had just witnessed one of my friends crushed by lighting."

"I don't know. I read in this Reddit thread that sometimes you can go into total autopilot. Like, you could see your wife's hand get caught in a blender, and then just drive to work like nothing even happened, because your body is, like, it's eight a.m., time to go to work."

"What Reddit thread is this?"

"One I was on looking up how to fix the blender."

Brian picks up his lacrosse stick and holds it up, daring me to toss in my shoe. I do, and he catches it easily. I know that there's supposed to be some primal Hatfield and McCoy–level rivalry between the performing arts kids and the jocks, but I am just as impressed with the way Brian can be looking at me and catching something in a tiny net above his head as I am when Essie gives one of her best onstage performances.

"I took your advice with Allison, by the way," he says, spinning the stick in his hands while keeping the shoe lodged in the net, another impressive feat. I'm also amazed he's managed to avoid all of the picture frames around us in the narrow hallway.

"Seriously? That's great, Brian, really. You know I think she's great, but you both are looking for such different things. It'll be so much less stressful for both of you if you're back to just being friends."

Brian stops what he's doing and looks at me blankly.

"I told her I love her."

"Why . . . why would you do that?"

"Because you said she was always talking about big romantic gestures, and all I wanted was something casual during lacrosse season."

"Correct. You want two completely different things. That's why I told you I thought it would be better if you broke up."

"Oh. Huh. You know I was trying to get Kilo tickets when we were talking the other day. It's possible that I maybe only heard the first half."

I dig the heels of my hands into my eyes and stifle the urge to shriek in frustration. Not that that's something Brian hasn't witnessed me do before, but I'm a little worried that with this on top of the frustration from the staple gun situation, if I start letting it out, I might never stop.

"Even accounting for your stunning lack of active listening powers, if you heard, and even *registered*, the first part about wanting totally different things—which is fine, by the way—why would you think the solution would be to tell her that you love her?"

"Because that's a romantic gesture. Which you said she wanted."

I pinch the bridge of my nose. I've never felt this move to be helpful or cathartic in any way, but I've seen so many people do it in movies and TV shows that I'm still holding out hope it could be useful.

"It's only romantic if you mean it. Otherwise it's just a really mean lie that's going to hurt her when she finds out you *didn't* mean it."

"But I do mean it. I mean, I think she's super nice and hot. So."

"And when you decide you want to be single in, like, three weeks, like you always do about a month into a relationship, you're going to tell her . . ."

"That since she's so nice and superhot, she'll find another guy to tell her she loves her in, like, a week." He gestures toward the door, like the line of guys waiting to confess their love for Allison might be right outside the door. He looks slightly confused at my exasperation, like he's not sure what part of his plan might need further explanation.

Every day I pray my brother doesn't find the men's rights activist board on Reddit. Not because I think he's going to be sucked in and become a raging misogynist or anything, but because he'll say shit like this with all sweetness and sincerity, and they'll think he's on their side.

"You should break up with Allison," I say, mostly to the floor or my shoes, as I march up the stairs past my brother.

"I don't know, Mia. After I just told her I love her? Seems kind of cold. But listen, could you help me out with asking her to homecoming? I was thinking I'd do the thing where I spell it out in cupcakes, but I'm not sure if she spells her name with an *i* or a *y*, and I feel like she might get mad if I ask."

I close the door to my bedroom before he can finish his question. I don't slam it because, honestly, I probably will attempt to advise him on his homecoming gesture. No cupcakes, though, because that's actually how Allison's ex asked her to prom last year, but something simpler, like a sweet note left in her locker and maybe, *maybe* a balloon. But he'll probably go with the cupcakes anyway.

My phone buzzes with a rapid series of photos—Essie's arm, bandaged and arranged on a fuzzy pillow; Talley fanning her with what looked like one of his little brother Jack's giant books on dinosaurs; Jack wearing a toy stethoscope checking for Essie's very important elbow heartbeat.

I text Essie.

Taking the day tomorrow for rest and iron consumption?

I don't like kale.

You like lying down and watching ten straight hours of Grey's Anatomy.

That was before. Now I associate hospitals with trauma.

Your favorite character is literally a trauma surgeon.

Yeah, but now I really get it.

> Do you promise to leave all the tools alone from now on? And in general listen to me when I'm trying to help you avoid getting maimed?

> You can't contain me, Mia. I'm a wild spirit. Can't be tamed. Sometimes I just have to live life.

> Good epitaph. Little long for a tombstone though. I'll make sure it gets on the prayer card.

Essie sends me a tongue-sticking-out emoji, and I toss my phone on the bed.

It's not like I think I know everything. But I do know some things, and the fact that all my efforts to impart wisdom or caution to my friends and family always fail is getting old.

I thought things might change this year. Senior year. The year I become more than some lowly techie, seamlessly blending into the black curtain with my all-black outfit (and thus easily ignored). The year I become *stage manager*. The person in charge of everything. Some people might argue that the person in charge of everything is the director, but they'd be wrong. A director is looking at acting choices: emotions and tone and blocking. Important, in the scheme of the theatrical arts and all. But the stage manager is the one scream whispering over the backstage mics,

"You're on." And if you have to choose between the importance of how someone is saying their lines onstage or whether they are actually, physically onstage instead of in the bathroom, the latter is going to win out.

But apparently my new title didn't magically gift me with any new authority. It's not like I'm power hungry or anything. I don't want to reign over the actors like I've seen some stage managers do. (Liam K., stage manager from my sophomore year, actually made everyone call him "sir.") It's just occasionally, occasionally, it would be nice to know that they know that I know stuff. Which I do. I got to shadow a real professional techie during spring break last year who works at our local touring theater. And it was amazing. Not just the way the tech crew kept everything moving onstage, but the way they organized the props backstage, and Jason, the guy I was shadowing, even stopped an actor from leaving the wings with their skirt tucked into their underwear. And no one but me and the actor knew that it was Jason who saved the most emotional scene in the whole show from unintentionally becoming a broad comedy moment. I saw the show the next night, and every time the audience gasped or sighed, I thought about the people they couldn't see who were responsible for that joy, that shock, that thrill. Who don't get to come out for bows. I still email him sometimes if I have a question about the light board, and he always answers me. It felt good to think he thought I was important enough, or maybe just serious enough, to mentor.

I've watched the video manuals for every one of our tools, too. I have an actual body of knowledge. And yet, when I try to gently, so gently, explain to my own crew that's not really the best way to hold a power drill, I know they're not really listening to me. It reminds me of the look in our physics teacher Mr. Robert's eyes when he realizes that our class, like all the classes before us, is not really absorbing the science thing he's teaching us. This slow resignation and disappointment. Sympathy for the poor man's broken spirit had me watching YouTube videos on entropy, just so I was confident enough to ask a question. Because eventually if you realize no one's ever listening to you, you might start to question whether you exist at all.

My phone buzzes again, this time with a FaceTime call. I answer it, and instead of Essie's face filling up the screen, it's her arm.

"It's throbbing," she whines.

"You're not getting any sympathy from me."

"What about brownies?"

"I will maybe make you brownies. But only as a stealth delivery system for iron."

"I don't want kale brownies."

"You won't even be able to tell the difference."

"I'm thinking of becoming a nurse," I hear Talley's disembodied voice call out from somewhere behind Essie.

"Talley, you gagged basically uncontrollably when we had the first-aid unit in health," I point out.

"True. But I feel this could be a turning point in my life. This is the moment. My stomach is now as strong as my resolve."

"Essie, could you open the picture I just sent you and point the phone at Talley," I ask, closing the search window for "wound + pus."

"What the f—" Talley's cursing is preempted by a dry heave.

"I don't think the medical profession is for you, babe," Essie says, not unkindly, as Talley continues to make retching noises.

"What do you think Mr. L is going to do to us tomorrow?" Essie asks, making our mild-mannered drama teacher sound way more intimidating than he is. The last time blood was shed on our stage while he was gone (at last year's spring musical set breakdown, Cathy cut her arm on a—thank god, already turned off—electric saw, because no one listened when I said you should cover the tools before starting on anything else), he made us read and analyze *Oedipus*. I'm not sure edification being used as punishment is setting us up to be lifelong learners or anything, but at least he doesn't believe in giving detention. It conflicts with rehearsal, after all.

"Maybe he'll make you remove all the staples connecting the old set by yourself. And, for obvious reasons, one-handed," Talley suggested.

"You don't think he'll actually make me audition tomorrow, do you?" she asks, eyes suddenly wide.

"Well, Ms. Delty, I would understand if you had injured your mouth, but I have seen actors go onstage with fresh, not-yet-splinted breaks, and if you want to make it in this industry . . ." Talley says, in his best impression of our drama teacher. Mr. L talks a lot about what it takes to make it in the acting industry, which apparently includes hard work, dedication, perseverance, and, if possible, the ability to move seamlessly between posh and cockney accents.

"Why are you worried about an audition? Especially an audition for *A Christmas Carol*?" I ask, genuinely puzzled at Essie's sudden show of anxiety. Not only is she, even forgetting the best friend bias, the best actor in the whole school—she landed a lead sophomore year, which is basically unheard of—*A Christmas Carol* is put on mainly as a fundraiser for the spring production. Not even the most serious, New York City–bound drama kids see it as anything but an excuse to wear some interesting

Victorian costumes and have a semi-legitimate excuse to procrastinate on end-of-the-semester projects.

"I'm auditioning for . . . an unexpected role," Essie mumbles. I sit up straight. Essie is not a mumbler. She is both committed to all her ideas and opinions *and* deeply invested in the importance of enunciating. For a moment I'm worried that Talley gave her a combination of pain meds and sugar-free gum that has caused some kind of rare but life-threatening allergic reaction.

"You don't want to be Mrs. Cratchit?" I ask. Normally, Mrs. Cratchit, as the matriarch of the play, goes to the star senior girl. There are always outliers though; last year Cassidy Blanch had auditioned for and was cast as the Ghost of Christmas Present, because her girlfriend was auditioning for the Ghost of Christmas Past and she thought it was cute. And we've had a couple of gender-bent Scrooges.

"I want to be the Ghost of Christmas Yet to Come," she says, making direct eye contact with the iPhone's camera.

I'm stunned.

"That's not . . . a speaking role. It's a pointing role . . . which, granted, would be difficult in your current slinged state," I say.

"The sling will be off by the time we start rehearsals."

"But why? You love speaking."

"I want to push myself as an actor," Essie says, tossing her hair a little in what I think is supposed to be haughty indifference, but doesn't quite land when she strains her arm and winces.

"And . . ." Talley prompts.

"And I want to challenge how other people see me."

"Which will be quantified by . . ." Talley prompts again, looking delighted at trying to get Essie to say something out loud she'd obviously prefer to be left unsaid.

"And I want to see if I can own it enough that I get the first-ever Nutmeg Award for a nonspeaking part," she says, the whine back in her voice.

"Ah," I say. I guess it must be hard to top getting the Nutmeg Award, the coveted Oscar of all public high schools in central Connecticut, in her junior year. It's admirable, really.

"How exactly are you going to do wordless acting from under a black shroud?" I ask.

"I . . . have not quite figured that out yet, but I know something will come to me," Essie says. "Okay, this whole conversation has been exhausting, and I am weak with blood loss. Mia?"

"I will bake you the brownies. With a side of kale. Which you would eat if you understood the importance of nutrition, or balance, or the wisdom of your best friend."

"We love you, Mia," Essie says, as I hear Talley shout, "So, so much."

I end the call. I know my friends love me. But I also know they're rarely listening.

I lie back on my bed, staring at my phone. I should not go on ReelLife. I have homework and some things to put together for auditions tomorrow, and yesterday on the time-suck app, I watched a video about how the dust under your bed can mix with your hair and trash and eventually gain sentience, and even though I'm pretty sure it was someone's film school project and not a *Crash Course* episode or anything, I did take it as a sign I should probably dust. I open the app anyway.

I like to bookmark actual helpful videos that I'm never actually going to use to make it at least *feel* like I'm being proactive. Totally going to bake that apple cake. That's a braid style I could wear tomorrow. I bet I could become bilingual if I followed these ten easy steps for success. I flick to the next video. It's someone with an extensive voice and face filter on, so a CGI-looking fairy-goddess head is superimposed on her not-so-fairy-like torso (though maybe fairy goddesses wear slightly rumpled white button-downs, what do I know), and their voice is altered so it's both super echoey and kind of musical. They're obviously going for a wise vibe.

"Hello, friends. Today CheetahCheeater asked, 'What should I do if a friend is dating someone who is constantly putting her down, but she doesn't see just how cruel he's being?'" CGI fairy goddess sadly (and wisely) shakes her head. "I can see how that would be difficult for you. It's hard to see a friend in pain. But what we must understand is, no matter the sting in the moment, pain is what makes us stronger; strong enough to be the person we need to be. Though you might not make sense of it now, the pain your friend is going through is part of her journey through this universe. By trying to stop it, you will rob her of this important time to fortify herself, to become the fantastically strong woman she's destined to be. Thank you for trusting me with this question."

This is the worse piece of advice I've ever heard. Let some dick emotionally abuse your friend because it'll make them strong? How about letting them know they're strong and wonderful right at this moment, and don't deserve to spend any time with someone who doesn't see it? Or, if you want to be more strategic about it, how about organizing one of those PowerPoint parties, and you assign each of your friends an asshole of cinema, and while they're giving their presentations, you look at the friend dating the dick pointedly until she realizes she has to leave him? *That* would be a solid piece of advice.

Whatever filter makes the person's hair seem to blow gently in the breeze is impressive, but I don't think that's going to trick anyone into thinking this person is actually wise. Except . . . I click into the comment section and scroll. An endless stream of "So true" and "You always have the right answer" and "Preach."

I swipe into her profile: 120,000 followers. That's twice the population of my entire town. And we're not even a quaint, *Gilmore Girls*–size Connecticut town. We're big enough for a downtown *and* an uptown Trader Joe's, and they're both always crowded.

And even figuring in that there might be people following just to rage watch or mock, or bots, or people who maybe saw the one video that did offer some advice worth following and then never thought about the account again . . . that is still so many people listening to this person's advice.

I don't think I've ever been jealous of a follower count before. Fame has always seemed terrifying to me, a mix of eyes always focused on you and so many sets of possibly conflicting expectations from people you've never met, who think they know you. Who think you owe them something.

But wouldn't it be cool to have that many people value what you have to say? Having that many people you can help?

I flip to my own profile: 102 followers, mostly people from Essie's theater camp who are very, very invested in following back. I've never actually made a video. What's the point in shouting into a black hole? What if I sounded ridiculous or accidentally insulted someone? I flip back to WisdomofGaia32 and scroll through their thumbnails. I expect to see something without the filter, a video of their crystal haul, them playing with a cute kid or animal, an apology or explanation or call to action they think needs to be done with their actual face. I scroll and scroll, but the hundreds of videos offer no proof that this person is not actually a mystical fairy who entered our world and immediately bought an iPhone and offered their unqualified advice. No one knows who they are. But they trust them anyway.

"I could do that."

It's a thought that just comes to me. Maybe no one in my real life will listen to my advice, but if I was just some random mysterious voice on the internet, some internet people might listen. Some internet people might be helped. I fiddle with the app for a few minutes and find there isn't a way to make two profiles on one account. Deleting my profile completely, then the app, was easy. Maybe I didn't even do it so I could create some online persona. Maybe I was just finally being responsible and would start working on my physics homework instead of scrolling.

The sense of responsibility lasts about five minutes. I pause for a moment over the question of username. Maybe a pun, to seem jokey and approachable, like I wasn't taking myself too seriously? Or a literary allusion, so I seem well-read? I finally go with HeretoHelp. Not my wittiest, but I figure I should probably save my moments of brilliance for the actual advice, right?

As soon as I'm in on the new account, I tap into the filter options. The filters are a new feature added a few months ago. At first people just used them to add a joke that needed a talking T. rex or a troll, but pretty quickly new accounts were popping up with people using them to be anonymous. Unfortunately, that's mostly because they want to say super-offensive stuff without someone telling their boss (or honestly, their mom) they're a bigot. But there are still plenty of people who use them for dramatic effect, like Gaia. Or, if the rumors are true, some super-popular creators in everything from cooking accounts to BookTok have set up anonymized profiles to try stuff out, or maybe even see if people like what they have to say, or just like how they look in front of the camera. There's a kind of game made out of it now, trying to figure out if the bunny or the glowing ball of light is your favorite creator in disguise.

I flip though the filter options. I don't want to be an animal or a mystic creature. I briefly consider the blur feature, that just makes your moving image hazy enough that not even your parents would be able to identify the swishing colors as you, but watching that for too long always makes me a little dizzy.

Shimmery, haloed color filters all cloak a bit, but don't fully anonymize. And then there's the void filter. It makes you a kind of translucent human shape moving in a totally black space. Maybe it's poetic, speaking into the void as a void. Or maybe if I was actually doing my homework, I'd learn that both being in a void and *being* a void simultaneously should, by the laws of physics, mean I cease to exist. Still, I like the idea of it.

I select void mode and a voice modulator pretty close to Gaia's, maybe a little more "shout down a tunnel" and less "I'm speaking to you from another plane." I wish I had one of the stands Essie has when she's making videos, but instead I just use some strategically placed book piles until I have the phone's camera pointing at me, the red button in the center pulsing and letting me know it's ready to record. The tiny square version of me in the bottom left is already void me. I do a few arms flaps and the YMCA to make sure it is, in fact, matching my movements, though I guess I won't actually be doing a lot of arm moving in the videos. All that's left to do now is . . . figure out what I want to say. What wisdom I want to impart. I'm temporarily paralyzed until I realize it will be reaching basically no one. I think about all the times my tips went unheeded, minus the whole "don't touch the power tools" thing, which I figure is a little too niche. Or, I guess—based on some of the more gruesome DIY home-improvement Reddit threads Brian has read to me—isn't niche, but would still go under the most ignored category of advice given by anyone. And even though I'm going to give advice to no one, really—I still want to say something worth hearing.

I mentally flip through my greatest hits, as far as attempted drama club interventions, before I remember one that I think could actually be useful. After auditions last spring, I found one of the tinier freshmen practically hyperventilating in the bathroom. After getting her to breathe, she told me that she was worried that by doing drama instead of soccer, something she'd been filling her afternoons with since third grade, she'd drift apart from her two best friends, who were still soccering, until, and these are her exact words, "one of them gets pregnant, and I hear about it from just, like, normal gossip." She then very frantically clarified that she doesn't think one of them would get pregnant, then frantically further clarified if they did, she would never slut shame them and just would want to be there to help, but she couldn't if they had drifted.

I explained to her that having friends in different extracurriculars was great, and that even though my best friends were in drama and band, they still managed to be extraordinarily codependent, and that even though theater kids made up a solid percentage of my social circle, having the jock friends I made through Brian meant I would hang out with people who saw the world (or at least, the world of high school) in a different light.

Which was important and refreshing and all that. When she still looked a little shaky, I told her she could join the spirit committee that always fills the soccer and lacrosse team members' lockers with baked goods on game day, so her friends would know she was still thinking of them, and she could invite them to set build days. That's how you give advice—one part big picture, one part something actionable. I thought she was really listening, too, with these giant watery eyes that made her look like a baby animal so adorable it goes viral. But when I finally finished explaining this solid-gold plan, she just said, "I bet if I ask the coach today, I could go through the last few days of tryouts, and at least stay on the reserve team!" She did thank me, which was nice, if slightly insulting after she had ignored everything I said. I wasn't being thanked for my actual advice, just for being a human someone could talk at until they worked things out on their own. Which I know is sometimes all people need, but after it happens more than a dozen times, you begin to wonder what it says about you that you could so easily be replaced with a mannequin.

But still—this was a solid bit of advice I hadn't forgotten. And just because one admittedly distraught freshman hadn't used it, who's to say someone else who was in a calmer mental state wouldn't?

I sit up straight, which isn't something I think will actually register on void mode but makes me feel more professional, and hit record.

"Realizing you're not passionate about what your friend is anymore, even if that's what brought you together in the first place, doesn't mean your friendship is over," I start, then hit pause.

I stare at the phone until the screen goes to sleep and I'm faced with my own reflection. Is this pathetic? Hoping strangers will listen to me because my friends don't? Is it more pathetic just to accept that I'll never be listened to by anyone? Is it pathetic that I'm agonizing this much about posting a video that I've already established will most likely be seen by no one? Do I think that if I keep posing rhetorical questions, I can philosophize forever and avoid making any actual decisions?

I flop back on my bed and stare at my ceiling. The dolphin mobile that's been hanging above my bed since I was eight spins lazily. A present from Brian, the first Christmas Dad gave us $20 each and told us we were responsible for getting gifts for each other at the annual community craft fair. According to Dad, he had tried to point out to Brian the fact that mobiles were usually given as gifts to babies, but Brian had successfully countered that I liked dolphins, and though I probably didn't spend quite as much time staring at the ceiling as an infant did, I definitely spent some time looking up from my bed and was more likely than a baby to get bored if there wasn't anything up there to look at besides water stains and spider guts. And he was right. It was something I always appreciated about my brother: for all his obliviousness in matters of his love life, he had the ability to look at a series of facts and come to a conclusion based on those facts only—not how someone else might perceive the conclusion. It's why he started wearing his lacrosse helmet in the car when being driven around by his friends after he read a statistic about crashes caused by teen drivers.

I stared up at Rosaline the dolphin (named by Essie during one of her Shakespeare eras). What would Brian do? Maybe it wasn't the best question to ask as I pondered whether I should convince strangers to listen to my advice. But even the tech bros on podcasts, who definitely think they know everything, always have, like, some kind of role model. Everyone's looking to someone for guidance. So why not Brian as mine? And if I were Brian, I think I'd ask, "Why not me?"

I sit up, grab my phone, and finish recording the video. Before I can change my mind, I hit post.

Probably nothing would come from it. But I think I'd regret it if I didn't try.

THREE

"Is everyone here for the three-thirty audition time slot?" I ask.

Nods, with everything from energized excitement to just-as-energized terror behind them, from the assembled group of freshmen. We don't really do any hazing in drama, because hazing is super fucked up. But it is a well-respected tradition that all non-freshmen start circulating the rumor, as early in the school year as possible, that rather than being a nothing show, *A Christmas Carol,* specifically your first *Christmas Carol* audition, is the thing that will set your drama club future in stone. The truth is freshmen are all relegated to single-line Cratchit children, and how big a group we get every year determines just how big of an asshole Scrooge seems for paying poor Bob Cratchit so little. It's a little mean, maybe, but it's stress doled out equally, at least. The funniest part is we have somehow collectively kept the plot from Mr. L for years, which means he has no idea why the freshmen are all acting for their lives at these tryouts.

"All right, everyone can hang out here until I call your name: you'll come in, give your monologue, and you're dismissed as soon as you're done. You'll be called in groups of four, and you might be asked to read in pairs too. Cast list will be posted tomorrow by the band room before first period."

The band room thing is what I think of as Mr. L's hazing ritual, though he thinks it's just a relevant test in listening—even though I have witnessed stage managers from the past three years very clearly state the cast list would be posted by the band room on the west side of the school instead of the east-side drama room, about half of the freshmen will show up backstage tomorrow morning looking terribly confused.

"Glen Friedman, Ally Taub, Kelly Mica, Ann Baker," I call, holding the door to the drama room open as the freshmen shuffle in, some faking confidence, others looking practically green.

I head backstage while the actual auditioning is going on. One of the perks of being the stage manager is I might have to organize and corral during the whole process, but I don't have to watch dozens of monologues from *The Glass Menagerie*. Not that I don't care about the process. I love watching the show going from words on the page to the shaky, overacted scenes of rehearsal, to something that tears the audience's attention away from whatever was filling their heads when the lights go down. I just don't like to see everyone so panicked. There's nothing quite so stressful as stressed-out people I can't do anything for. And after four years of this, I know the only advice worth giving is "Try to remember that no one has ever died from a bad audition" and "Definitely do not google whether or not that's true" when I leave.

I fall heavily into the biggest beanbag in the corner of the back-stage. I'm just about to get my algebra homework out, because having the notebook open in front of me is the first step in not procrastinating so much that I'll end up doing differential equations in the bathroom before first and second periods, when a shadow falls over me.

"Anyone sitting here?" The shadow owner, a tall girl wearing black skinny jeans, asks, gesturing to the neighboring beanbag. But her question throws me. I shake my head no, because it's true that no one is sitting there and I try to be an honest person, but it's such a bizarre question, I can't form an answer verbally. It would be like if someone broke into my bedroom and asked me if anyone was sitting here, on the edge of my bed. No, but more importantly, who are you, and why do you think this is a place that you can sit?

"Sorry, is this just a place theater people hang out?" she continues, already looking completely at ease as she sprawls out onto the beanbag chair. The general confusion and slight social-awkwardness-induced horror must show on my face.

"Basically," I say. I know Talley and Essie would have corrected her, would say this was a place where theater people make art, connect people on a visceral level, turn words on the page into mesmerizing spectacle. But despite my love for every production we've put on here, I know this is also a place where my friend stapled a flyer to her arm, so I don't think we have to be too precious about it.

"Well, thanks for not kicking me out. I'm waiting for my ride, and your school's very under-attended art club is putting up a mural outside, and I really didn't want to be tapped to help," she says.

John Adams High isn't so small that I ever feel like I *know*-know everyone, but it *is* small enough that by senior year, every face that's not a tiny freshman face seems semi-familiar. Hers is not. She's completely stunning, with long black wavy hair that's so dark it has that kind of blue shine, pale skin, and deep brown eyes. It always irks me a little when people assume ace people can't identify attractive individuals, like that's our version of color blindness or something. I can see beautiful landscapes and beautiful paintings and beautiful people.

"Uh—" I have a lot of questions, so I just settle on my first. "Are you new here?"

"I like to think me being new technically expired after the first month of school, because that's around the same time I had the lunch schedule down. Very impressed with the vegan option on Friday, by the way. But I did go to another school in my younger years." She smiles in a conspiratorial way—a way that makes me wish we were conspiring together, and I smile back as if on instinct. I'm used to talking with very confident people—drama is really a pretty even mix of people who think they're amazing and people hoping to become amazing. But I wasn't sure I had ever talked with someone my age who seemed so comfortable with themselves.

"Mia!" Essie's voice carries across the backstage. It must be time for an audition-round shift, even though it hasn't felt like half an hour. I should have put an alarm on my phone.

"I'll be right back," I say, though I'm not entirely sure why. We haven't even exchanged names, so it's not like I owe her an explanation of my schedule. I'm just kind of hoping she'll still be there when I return.

I head over to Essie, who's wearing a fuzzy cloud-printed robe in what is supposedly an effort to stay warm without anything touching her sling, but I know is really so she looks as injured and forlorn as possible while still at school.

"They ready for a new round?" I ask.

"No idea. Why are you talking to Sadie?"

"Who?"

"The girl on the beanbag. The drama club beanbag, which she shouldn't be on anyway."

"It's not a big deal. Joey Kossy sits there all the time."

"Joey Kossy is dating Mike, who is in drama. There's a connection. There's a reason," Essie says, looking at Sadie warily, a look that's normally reserved for people she's worried might take her part.

"Did you hear she's trying out or something? Because she told me she's just waiting for a ride."

"You haven't heard about her?"

I stare at her, letting the silence remind her that my main source of hearing about people is Essie herself.

"Sadie. Sadie McCrew. The piano prodigy?"

"Nope. No idea. But if she was really a piano prodigy, wouldn't she be at the Academy?" I ask. The Academy, our local arts magnet school, has turned out multiple Grammy winners and members of various philharmonics, according to our town paper and local news segments.

"She *was* at the Academy. Until she got *asked to leave*," Essie says, adding the last part in a dramatic whisper.

"You mean expelled?"

"Well, apparently you can't actually legally expel someone from high school for having a cursed vagina," Essie says.

Sometime after her third summer at theater camp, Essie stopped being confused by truly strange, confounding things. But I still balk a little when I hear about a mix of witchcraft and genitalia.

"A what?"

"You heard me. Crissy, you know my friend from voice lessons? Her sister plays flute at the Academy, and she said not one, not two, but *six* separate students over the course of three years had these weird freak accidents during performances right after hooking up with Sadie, and—"

"If Academy kids died, or were maimed even, we would have heard about it," I say. "It would have been on the news. And if they had some kind of *Final Destination* thing going on, I think it would have just been shut down."

"They didn't die or get that hurt, but they'd, like, get their tongue stuck in a tuba or something, which I know doesn't sound like it would be so uncommon, but it is if you've been tuba-ing ten hours a day for basically your entire life. Once everyone started connecting the dots between the accidents and spending alone time with Sadie—"

"You cannot go from saying 'cursed vagina' to 'alone time' in a single conversation."

"I'm layered. By the time they put it together, people seemed to think that just being near Sadie, even without anything our lord and savior would disapprove of, might be enough to hex you. And so the school administrators asked her not to come back for her senior year, as her presence might have caused an uncomfortable environment for the other students."

"I still don't think actual adults would make a call like that about someone's future based on some kind of supernatural rumors," I say, trying to subtly steal another glance of Sadie.

"Right, because that would be the most fucked-up thing a principal has ever done," Essie says, dripping with sarcasm. She has a point. Last spring they caught the principal two towns over betting on the JV basketball games—against his own school's team—and rigging the championship by giving the two star players suspensions. I think they're going to make a podcast about him.

"Okay. Rumor transmitted. I'm going to go try to get some homework done if you don't have any stories of, like, a guy who makes you fail math tests with his penis or something," I say.

"You're not actually going back to talk with her?"

"Yes. For several reasons. Curses are fake. Having to transfer your senior year because of something fake sucks, and so I'm not going to add low-key bullying to the sucky things in her life. And even, even if curses were real, which they are not, I'm pretty safe from hookup-related curses."

"Okay," says Essie, her eyes still narrowed but easing a bit at my reassurance.

"Also, I love you, but you didn't really seem convinced until you remembered I wouldn't be making out with the cursed vagina owner, and I'm very disappointed in you."

"Ugh. Fine. You talk to her, see if she's cool. If she's worth knowing, I'll tell everyone in drama to extend the hand of friendship or whatever. But I'm not risking a cursed production if she's an asshole. Fair?"

I'm not sure if it is fair, but it is a concession, which can be hard to wrest from Essie, so I nod and watch her walk back to the auditions. I know she was just trying to say she'd help, but I also think she might be overestimating her power over drama club if she thinks her word alone could get them to overlook the threat of a curse. She couldn't even convince the drama treasurer to increase the makeup budget enough to replace our old stock with only cruelty-free stuff—not that I would ever bring up that painful loss, even on a nothing audition day.

"I'm back. Oh, and I'm Mia," I say to Sadie, trying to sit down in the beanbag chair a little more gracefully since there's an audience now (I'm not successful).

"I'm Sadie. But I'm guessing from all the looks you and your friend were giving me, you already knew that," she says. I want to run away and hide under a rock, but she doesn't look mad. I search for something to say that will make the fact that she caught us gossiping about her better, and come up with nothing. Luckily, she interrupts my floundering.

"It's okay. It's a good story. Sex, shame, someone swallowing two whole pieces of their clarinet onstage. I like telling it too," she says, easily. I'm starting to think she might say everything easily. It's such a change from the frantic energy of drama club or even Brian and his lacrosse friends. I want her to teach me how to be that at ease with another person. Or maybe with myself.

"It's super fucked up that they kicked you out for something that isn't possibly true," I say, deciding that the best course of action is probably to assure her I'm not someone who actually believes in curses.

"Honestly? It was more logistically annoying than anything else. I wasn't bullied; my friends are still my friends. It's just the pool of people willing to make out with me had dwindled down to nothing, and I never had time with our crazy rehearsal schedule to meet someone who wasn't at the Academy. I mean, sex isn't everything, but I like to at least think that something might be able to happen, you know? Just to keep a little hope alive? But, based on the side-eye I've been getting here, it looks like I'm going to have to wait until college." She lets out a big sigh. "More time to practice, I guess."

I feel my eyes grow big as I wonder what kind of advanced sex practicing she can do alone when I realize she's probably talking about the piano.

"So, you don't actually have a cursed vagina, so that's one rumor dispelled, but are you actually a child prodigy? Or, I guess, a teenage prodigy?" I hope she won't feel too insulted I just called her a child. But I've never actually heard of a teenage prodigy. I wonder if that's because it's always going to seem more impressive to see a kid playing the piano who can't reach the pedals, or because by the time they're a teenager, they've evolved into being called a virtuoso or something like a piano Pokémon.

"That's what all the local news stories say, and Channel Six can't be wrong, right?" She blows a strand of hair out of her eyes. I can't tell if this is an extension of her nonchalance, or if she's trying to mask her annoyance at my question, but for some reason, I decide to keep going. It might make me a terrible person, but I don't think she's really in a position to be refusing even the possibility of friendship, even if it might be an annoying one like mine. So I kind of have free rein here.

"So, what's that like? The whole prodigy thing, I mean?"

"Way easier to make the teacher think I've been practicing, even if I haven't. Got to meet Yo-Yo Ma once—that was cool. And my parents are so terrified that the pressure of becoming the next Clara Schumann will lead me to a nervous breakdown, they've been making me take self-care breaks since I was, like, four, so I have very moisturized skin and a wide variety of meditation apps." She smiles, and I smile back but don't say anything. I'm waiting for a real answer. I can tell she knows it by the way she stares back at me and smiles slowly, like she's figured me out. Or maybe she's realized that I've figured her out.

"I love the piano. And I'm good at it, and other people tell me I'm good at it, which is a nice bonus, but that doesn't really matter because I know it. I know that in a year and five years and ten years, I want to be playing the piano, and barring some kind of hand-crushing incident, it looks like I'm going to be able to. And before you say it, I know even mentioning the hand-crushing incident seems like tempting fate, but I figure with a story like that, I could make a decent living as an inspirational speaker, talking about how when life gives you finger splints, or something like that."

She wiggles her hands as if to demonstrate how, for the moment, they're not broken. Her fingers are long and thin, and her nails are super short and painted jet black with little flecks of silver glitter. She's wearing a ring that's braided with gold and maybe copper, and I wonder if she has to take it off before she plays so it doesn't knock against the keys. Before I realize what I'm doing, I reach out and touch my finger to hers. I expect her to jerk away, but she doesn't, just smiles like strange girls touch her fingers all the time. Maybe they do. Maybe she has very eccentric piano groupies.

Thinking about piano groupies makes me realize I'm very possibly accidentally flirting. It's happened a handful of times, and it's never led to anything good. I know "leading someone on" is mostly a concept invented by people who feel entitled to sex and are trying to make you feel bad if you're not interested. But I also know it sucks when you think someone wants to be your friend, and it turns out they just actually want to be your lab partner, and I don't ever want to be the reason for someone's disappointment.

"I'm sorry, it's just, you were talking about hands—well, your hands— and I thought, they must be strong, like bodybuilder strong, but in your fingers, so I was curious about your, you know, finger muscles, but that's still super rude not to, you know, ask first."

"That's okay. We pianists are very proud of our finger muscles. But actually, if you really want to feel some serious prodigy strength, you've got to check out my wrists," she says, and before I can ask why, she's taken my hand and is guiding my fingers over her forearm. It is tight, and I can tell, in my limited-knowledge-of-anatomy sort of way, that there are powerful cords of muscles just beneath her freckly forearms.

I look up, and she's looking at me, and I realize this is not just a friendly demonstration of her strength. She wanted me to touch her arm, or maybe she wanted me *to want* to touch her arm. She wanted electricity to move from her skin to the tips of my fingers, just like I've read in all the romance books Essie insisted I go through back in middle school. And I'm not sad or upset or surprised that the electricity doesn't come. But I am a little surprised at the blush that creeps up my neck. This cool, confident person wants that spark with me. I suddenly flash to the two of us holding hands or, the piece of coupled intimacy I've always been the most jealous of, one of us walking into a room and someone calling out, "Hey, Sadie, where's Mia?" because we've truly become a pair.

Her phone buzzes, and she looks down at the screen.

"My ride's here. Thanks for letting me crash on theater turf," Sadie says.

She starts to get up to go, and I notice a tattoo of a curving staff of music starting at her knee and ending just before the top of her shorts.

"Is it a special song?" I ask, gesturing at the notes I never bothered to learn to read during my forced recorder lessons back in fourth grade.

"It is. And a pretty great tattoo origin story. But if I tell you all my secrets now, what will I have to offer next time?" she asks. She says it breezily, not the overly suggestive way I know Essie would. But not truly earnest either, like I would. She knows she has more to offer. I want her to offer it to me.

"Are you free on Saturday?" I find myself blurting out. Why did I say that? Am I free on Saturday? I just know I want to keep talking with her, and this seems like the next logical way.

"I have junior orchestra in the morning, but I'm free Saturday afternoon. Why?" She asks it in an obviously flirty way. Which probably means I should try to flirt back, which I know I don't have the skills to do. And should I explain that even though I very, very much want to spend all of Saturday doing whatever she wants to do, I'm really hoping that doesn't involve kissing?

"Do you want to go to the aquarium?" I ask. It's the least romantic place I can think of on the spot. Nothing but pools of great whites that remind you of your own mortality and a weird mix of Muzak and pop songs from when my parents were teenagers. Definitely not sexy.

"Sure. Here's my number," she says, ripping out a piece of notebook paper and scribbling her number down. "We can text about the details."

I watch her walk out the door, then look down at the paper—it's not loose-leaf, but actually blank music staffs, her number sitting on top of one. It makes me think of that documentary I watched once on people with synesthesia, when people can taste color and see sounds. I swear I can hear music as I watch her walk away.

FOUR

"You're going on a date with cursed Sadie," Essie says, her face slightly pixelated on FaceTime. It's times like these that I almost wish I was born during a less technological era, like the '90s. It seems like the benefit of talking on the phone should be that you don't have to worry about whatever face you're making when your best friend is piling lies on lies.

"It's not a date, she's not cursed, and there are no such thing as curses," I say, not even bothering to count them off.

"You don't take someone to the aquarium platonically," Talley is saying, gentler in his judgment than Essie but still definitive.

"And I'm just a humble scientist, but I think Sadie's bad-luck sex hexes have already gone way outside the official coincidence numbers," Essie says. It's amazing she's in AP chem at all.

"Even if I thought you were right about the curse, which you are not, I'm in no danger. Just your friendly neighborhood asexual over here, not hooking up with anyone."

"Mmm-kay," Essie says, obviously not believing me, but also obviously distracted by something else.

"Do you think I should get a tattoo over the staple scar?" she asks, holding up her arm. I can't tell if there will actually be a scar or not, as a third of her arm is covered in Band-Aids definitely not put there by a doctor.

"I thought you said you'd never get a tattoo because they take so many layers of make-up to cover up if you need to for a part," I point out.

"But if I'm going to be maimed anyway."

"You're not maimed," I say. "I could do some research on the best styles to cover scars, if you're really thinking about it—"

"Maybe we should get matching tattoos!" Essie says to Talley suddenly.

"With our anniversary?" Talley says.

"Guys. No. Do not get matching tattoos with your anniversary."

They both turn toward the camera, looking annoyed.

"Why not? Because you think we're going to break up?" Essie asks, icily, like I'm some adult who just pulled up the stats on teen marriage instead of the best friend who has always, always been in their corner.

"No, because you have, like, seven different anniversaries," I clarify, trying to make it sound light, like a joke, even though preventing them from doing this is super serious. "The one from seventh grade, the one from when you broke up and got back together in eighth grade, the ones that I keep telling you not to celebrate because you make the servers at Chili's uncomfortable—"

"It's not our fault we live in a society of prudes."

"You can't ask for a free brownie sundae to celebrate the anniversary of your first kiss, with tongue!"

"Talley, what do you think of this one?" Essie says, pointing to something on the screen that is obviously no longer my face.

"Yeah, no, that looks great. Plus, top of the foot, super coverable."

"No, wait," I say, and with some quick googling, I send them a link. "I remembered reading this, top of the foot is the most painful, and I think I saw this YouTube of a girl who went to an artist she found on Groupon and the needle severed a tendon, an important one, and now she can't walk without shooting foot pain."

"This one is glow in the dark," Essie says to Talley.

"Yo, Mia, dinner," I hear Brian shout. It seems almost unnecessary to tell them I have to go eat dinner, as they're obviously completely engrossed in planning out tattoos they will definitely regret before they turn twenty-one, but still, it is traditional to say goodbye before you get off the phone, and I believe in tradition.

"Okay, Brian's calling me for dinner. But to sum up: The tattoos are a bad idea, and I don't think tattoo removal is as complete as people seem to think it is. There's always, like, a ghost of a tattoo. Your bad decisions will be literally haunting you. Do you want to be haunted?"

"God, Mia, people get tattoos literally every day. There's probably more people getting tattoos right now then are having dinner," Essie says.

"And some people with high pain tolerances are probably doing both. Not everything is going to kill us."

I wave at them and end the call. I never said it was going to kill them. But there are a lot of things between a horrific death and sitting in your room safely watching Netflix. And they never seemed interested in letting me help them avoid the horrific-death-adjacent things.

As I walk down the stairs, I can hear the sound of "Don't You (Forget about Me)" playing from one of Dad's portable speakers, which makes me think tonight's dinner is going to be '80s themed. My father has a mild obsession with theme parties, but since raising two kids and working full time has meant less time to host "ragers" (his words, not mine), he's put that energy into weekly themed dinners. Besides being the main source of shareable photos I've had since middle school, it's also a pretty good way of deciding whether he's in the right mental space to ask for a favor. The month of "goth" dinners that involved covering whatever he made with poppy seeds and playing ghost noises off YouTube was apparently not a great month at the office.

By the time I get to the table, Mom and Brian are already there. Mom's hair is tied back with a giant neon-orange scrunchie, and Brian is wearing fingerless black gloves.

"You know, like the dude at the end," he says, lifting a fist up à la Judd Nelson.

"That dude is in the entirety of *The Breakfast Club*, not just the end," I point out, putting on the '80s accessory Dad has left by my plate, plastic bangle bracelets that look like they've been covered in glow-in-the-dark splattered paint.

"All right, everybody. We've got an exciting trip down memory lane for your mother and me, and an important history lesson for you two tonight," Dad says, putting down two steaming serving plates. He's wearing his favorite pants, gigantic ones printed with palm trees and stripes the color of rainbow sherbet. He actually wears them all the time, but since I know he's had them since college (a.k.a. the late '80s), at least now there's an excuse.

"Uh, Dad? I think the pudding is like . . . sneezing?" Brian says. I'm about to make a comment about the high rate of concussions among high school athletes when I notice that little bits of pudding *do* seem to be kind of exploding from the top of the dessert.

"Jesus, Rick, did you top it with Pop Rocks?" Mom asks, looking at the pudding with only slightly exasperated interest.

"Of course. I wasn't going to half-ass something as important as eighties night. It sets a bad example for the kids."

"And for the main course we've got . . ." I ask, looking at what appears to be perfectly normal steak tips, but the high rate of sci-fi movies I know Dad loves from the '80s makes me a little nervous.

"Steak. Bloody to feed your blood," he says, quoting *Moonstruck*, the rom-com that taught me the best way to let a stranger know you want to hook up is to listen to their most painful memory and make a kind of obvious metaphor about it.

"It is actually cooked well-done, though," Dad clarifies before sitting down, beaming at his latest curation.

"So. Who thinks they had the best day?" Dad asks. My mom once read in a parenting book, or maybe a blog post, that it's more effective to make day sharing into a kind of competition, rather than just a boring question. I think it's possible this is feeding into dangerous ideas about true joy only coming from winning, but who am I to argue with a child psychologist and/or mommy blogger?

"I'm pretty sure I aced my chem final," Brian says, beaming over a forkful of fried green tomatoes (an '80s movie I know my father hasn't even seen, but a movie title that's literally the name of a potential dinner dish is too good to pass up).

"How did you have a chem final? You're not even two months into the semester yet," I ask.

"Well, I decided to drop chem. So, it's like my chem final, you know?" Brian says, horrifyingly topping his steak with the Pop Rocks pudding and taking a giant fizzy bite.

"You're dropping chemistry? But you love science," Mom says. I want to clarify that Brian loves science fiction and has always been let down by the banality of mixing chemicals without accidentally producing a new (probably angry) life-form, but I'm too busy tentatively tasting the pudding.

"I was talking to Tommy the other day," Brian starts, spearing a few green beans on his fork (Dad has yet to clarify if the salad is on theme), "and he was saying, like, science is going to keep going whether I'm watching or not, right? Like, there are people our age who love science, and they're going to keep doing it no matter what. So if I'm not super obsessed with it, I figure I should try something new, and if I miss science, by the time I'm in college, I can just ask the science kids like, hey, what cool shit did I miss?"

"Sounds reasonable," Dad says, just before Mom starts to say something that would probably highlight the less-reasonable aspects.

"Mia, would you like to challenge?"

"Well, I met a cool person today. And we're going to the aquarium tomorrow."

"Great date spot," Brian says, in the voice of an astrology vlogger, spacey but still authoritative.

"It's not a date!" I say, possibly a little more defensively than I'd like, but this was now the third person trying to turn a casual platonic hang into something else.

"Cool. So it's a group thing," he says.

"No. It's just us."

"It's for, like, a school assignment? Or is your theater club doing one of those animal acting things, and you're getting a jump on 'being the stingray'?"

"No, I just, like I said, she's cool, so I asked her to go to the aquarium."

"You asked her on a date."

"You just think everything is a date."

"Mia, the aquarium is where I have made out with three of the most gorgeous girls in the senior class. Girls I know would not have let me hold their hand, if it wasn't for the exact lighting under the aqua tunnel. Gina Knight told me walking by the sharks reminded her of death, which made her feel more alive, which made her want to stick her tongue down my throat."

"Brian, I love that you feel so comfortable speaking so openly in front of us, but we are eating," Mom says with a slightly tired, but not disingenuous smile.

"Right, sorry, Mom. Anyway, Rachel Dent said she felt like she was in another world, before we, uh, had a moment with, you know, lips." Dad gives Brian a thumbs-up at his weirdly abstract description of first base.

"What I'm saying is," Brian continues valiantly, "the aquarium is, like, what people who make romantic movies think getting caught in the rain is. They got it kind of right—there is water involved. But there also needs to be stingrays."

I look from Brian to my parents, hoping they'll be able to explain, in detail, just how wrong he is.

"I had my first kiss by the sea lions. Eighth grade. Tim McDonnel," Mom says, a dreamy look in her eyes.

I turn to Dad.

"The year I taught the engineering after-school program, we took the kids to the aquarium as an end-of-the-year treat. It wasn't official, but a lot of parents did point to it for that summer's mini mono epidemic," Dad says.

"Mia, don't let anyone pressure you to do anything you don't want to do," Mom says, snapped out of her Tim McDonnel reverie. I nod. My parents have been very supportive and only a little confused since I came out as ace, though Mom seems to think this means I'm constantly being pursued by horny classmates I might not feel empowered to politely decline. The truth is me not being interested in kissing has never come up in such an immediate way.

"I'm still not sure sea creatures are as romantic as you all think they are, but I can handle myself either way," I reassure them.

I can handle myself is one of my most frequent lies, along with *I'm not worried*.

I'm about to expand on exactly how I will handle it if Sadie thinks this is a date, when "Day-O" comes up on the playlist, and we're all compelled to get up and perform the dance number from *Beetlejuice*, something we all know by heart because Dad has incorporated it not just into tonight's '80s theme, but all past dinners built around Halloween, the afterlife, and the filmography of Winona Ryder. It's corny, but I appreciate Dad's dedication to making the people he loves interact with the things he loves.

It makes me wonder if I'll have a group of people sitting around a kitchen table willing to do a silly dance because it makes me happy someday. I attempted to have a theater-themed thirteenth birthday party and asked everyone to come dressed as their favorite character, but Essie had actually convinced a lot of drama that making roles into "just costumes" was disrespectful to theater in general, while Talley told me he thought I was joking and Brian came dressed in all black, very sweetly misreading the instructions by coming as me. Maybe in college I could try instating themed dinners, dinners that would bond us forever and give us inside jokes for the next four years and beyond, and everyone would be grateful that I had put them on, bringing us together.

FIVE

Sadie is dressed for a date. I think. It's hard to tell when truly cool people are trying or not trying, fashion-wise. Essie has coordinated her nail polish to her phone case accidentally more than once. Meanwhile, the one time I attempted to tame my frizz with gel, whole flyaway chunks sprung up then, solidified, giving me a very unflattering spiked look I hadn't noticed until Talley successfully hung his key chain from one. So maybe the black body-con dress and aqua-blue drop earrings were just the first things Sadie saw as she was getting ready today for this: a platonic, get-to-know-you friendship outing, which is totally a thing that teenagers do, I'm sure of it.

"Hey. I got the tickets," I say, waving idiotically. I briefly consider asking her to Venmo me for hers, just to underline the overall non-date vibes, but I did ask her to come, and demanding payment for that seems wrong.

"Cool. Which animals do you want to stare at first? I vote whales."

"Because they sing?" I ask. She grins. I can tell from her expression my guess is wrong, but I still feel kind of powerful, being the cause of her genuine smile. I feel like a lot of the smiles I elicit from Talley and Essie teeter on the edge of pity. Like how you might smile at a dog who almost manages to roll over.

"I just think the belugas have the most human expressions. Which I guess is human-centric of me, but whatever," she says, and holds out her hand. I stare at it for a second. It is offered with all the confidence of habitual gesture, like there isn't even a question if I would grab it. So I do. Friends can hold hands. I don't hold my friends' hands, but that might just be because no one has offered theirs before. She doesn't lace her fingers through mine, which is a relief, as that feels almost painfully intimate. But as we pass by the penguins, she squeezes it lightly, before pointing out a baby one sliding across the ice. I wonder if people who see us think we're a couple. I wonder if being part of a couple feels like this, like being so connected you can share something with someone else without making a sound.

We reach the belugas and sit down on a bench in front of the tank.

"That's Tom," she says, pointing to a whale who seems to be semi-stuck to the front of the tank like a sucker fish.

"Officially, or . . ."

"I mean, officially, I'm sure he has a whale name from his whale mom. But that's what I call him."

"After . . ."

"He just looks like a Tom."

She stares at the whale and then flashes him two thumbs-ups.

"Sometimes I worry they aren't getting enough positive reinforcement," she explains. "I'd still just be a kid playing 'The Entertainer' over and over without sparkly stickers reminding me I'm great."

"You must have gotten a lot of stickers," I say, before scrambling for "Because of the, uh, virtuosity."

She smiles, still looking at the whale.

"I did. My dad loves telling this story about how once, when I was like five, he opened his briefcase and found his notepad covered in 'You're #1' stickers, and he was so touched by the fact I was trying to hype him up, he landed the biggest client of his career. But I was five, so I'm pretty sure my thought process went something like 'This paper is boring—if I add sparkly things, I can make it less boring.' Not 'Dad needs an ego boost.'"

"Did you tell him that?"

"No. It makes him happy. I don't know, I think it's kind of shitty to burst someone's bubble just because. Like, I have a cousin, and her dog died a few years ago, and now whenever she finds an old chew toy, she says that it's a sign from the dog from beyond. Why the hell would I try to take that away from her, even if it feels more likely it's just a misplaced toy?"

I nod. "Also, you know, I like the idea of kindly ghost dogs hanging around. Way more than ghost people. Maybe that's why squirrels sometimes dart up a tree out of nowhere. They're being chased by ghost dogs."

"Ghost dogs," she mutters.

I'm about to take it all back, explain that I didn't sleep well last night, when she grabs my hand on the bench and says, "That is absolutely brilliant. So many moments in my life that didn't make sense now have a perfect explanation—ghost dogs. Now, I know this is a little early in our relationship, but, Mia, do you want to get a ghost dog together?"

I have never wanted to get anything more in my life. I feel like I've just been granted membership into a club I didn't even apply to, and they have the best club sweatshirts, the kind that let you embroider your name on the front in cursive to show you're both seen as part of a group and as an individual. I have always been a little jealous of the sports and dance people who have those sweatshirts. I nod, a little giddy.

"Fantastic. What should we name them?" she asks.

"Tom Too," I say, nodding toward the tank. "But T-O-O, not the number."

"Of course. No one wants to be a number."

"It's why Thing One and Thing Two were so fucked up."

And then she's laughing, and I'm laughing too, and that's all I really remember, the wonderful sound of her laughter mixing with mine before suddenly her lips are on my lips. And then I shriek. I don't think I've ever shrieked before. I'm not really afraid of bugs. Also, I didn't think people shriek in the twenty-first century—I thought that was more a pre–Cold War kind of thing—but here I am, in front of the whales, not yelping or screaming but definitely shrieking.

I pull back and realize people are staring at us. I have no idea if Sadie is shocked or hurt or annoyed because I cannot look her in the face. I just stare at my thighs, then the ground, then mutter, "Going to the bathroom, be right back," and dash past the door marked with a skirt-clad shark.

I slam the stall door and let waves of hot embarrassment wash over me. There's so many layers of bad here. That Sadie definitely thought this was a date. That my first kiss was with someone I like so much and yet have 100 percent scared off forever. The shrieking. I briefly consider googling how to live in the bathroom of an aquarium. (Would it really be so different from what those kids did in *From the Mixed-Up Files of Mrs. Basil E. Frankweiler*?) But instead I make the more reasonable, if not more comfortable, choice of FaceTiming Essie.

"It's a date, isn't it?" is how she answers the phone.

"Gloating isn't very helpful," I say.

"I just had to get it out of the way. What happened?"

"How do you know something happened? Maybe I'm just calling to give you an update on how well things are going."

"Mia."

"She kissed me, and I shrieked and ran away."

"Because you know you're hexed now."

"No. Because . . ." Because it was surprising, and my life has had so little surprise in it, I have outsize reactions to it. Because after figuring out the whole ace thing, I had crossed "kissing" off the list of things to overthink, so now I had under-thought it.

"Did you like it?" Essie asks.

"I don't know. I kind of interrupted it. But . . . no fireworks."

"You know, I may have overhyped kissing, being a drama queen and all. It's not always going to be fireworks."

"I don't think I'd shriek if she did it again."

"Low bar. Did you even tell her you're ace?"

"It didn't come up."

"Well . . . it's up now."

"Maybe if I stay in here long enough, she'll leave," I suggest.

"Maybe if you stay in there long enough, she'll just come in to get you, and you'll have to explain yourself through the bathroom stall. Or she'll call for help, and you'll have to explain it to one of the aquarium educators."

"Essie," I begin, resting my forehead on the stall wall, even though that is super unhygienic, because that's how necessary making this moment a little more dramatic seemed to be. "I really like her."

"Awwww. Mia's first crush. Hold on . . . Okay, I screenshotted the important milestone to send Talley."

I want to tell her not to, and that for just a few minutes, I'd like her to be my friend, who she wants to help, instead of a source of entertainment for her and Talley. But that seems like a secondary issue at the moment.

"It's not a crush. I just want to hold her hand and maybe get a ghost dog together."

"That's what a crush is."

"But I don't want to suck her neck or anything."

"Je-sus Christ, I told Talley he has to stop sending you X-rated fanfics. Just talk to her. Talk to her about where you're at. And what you're into. Which is what literally everyone does when they're at the start of a new relationship."

I make some frustrated moan-wailing to let Essie know I hear her, and I know she's right, yet the prospect of actually doing that is terrifying. It occurs to me someone who doesn't know our shorthand, or that I'm on the phone, might think I'm in some sort of distress and call for help, and I'll end up talking to two aquarium educators, so I stop.

"It's also possible you're at the beginning of a really good story for Sadie to tell at the start of her next relationship," Essie continues. "Depending on how quickly you exit the bathroom, and how many sea creatures you scared with your screams."

I hadn't even thought of the poor sea creatures. I hope I was less startling than whatever they might encounter in the wild.

"Okay. I'm going to go. I'm going to go, and I'm going to talk it out. And everything will be fine."

Essie isn't saying anything, and I can tell from the way her eyes are flicking side to side, she's actually reading something on her phone.

"Essie. Essie!"

"Hmm?"

"Are you going to go call Talley and make fun of my ineptitude?"

"Oh, I've been texting him the whole time—he's coming over so I can better reenact it."

"I hate you both."

"And yet I'm still the first one you call."

"Habit. Very hard to break."

"Text me how it goes," she says before I hang up. I take a deep breath, check my shoes for any trailing toilet paper (just because you *think* you've hit rock bottom doesn't mean you actually have), and walk out.

"You okay?"

"Ah! Um, yes," I say, trying to cover up the fact that I'm startled by Sadie's position directly outside the bathroom door. I thought I had a few more steps to psych myself up.

"I didn't want to follow you in, but I also wanted to be close by in case you needed help. Because now I know, if you need to, you can scream," she says, smiling. I can't tell if her expression is concerned or annoyed, but I'm a little encouraged by the smile.

"That was the first time I did that."

"The shrieking?"

"The kissing."

"Oh. That's cool," Sadie says, as if it's a completely normal confession, not what I assume to be a pretty big statistical anomaly.

"I really didn't mean to shriek in your face."

"It's okay. One time my cousin thought she saw a spider on my nose and was so freaked out she punched me in the eye. While shrieking. So someone screaming in my face without detaching my retina is a big improvement." She rakes a hand through her hair as she laughs. She is so cool. It seems embarrassing to think a peer, a maybe friend, a maybe more than friend, is so intensely cool in the way I might think someone famous is intensely cool, but I figure it's only a matter of time before Sadie does become famous, so I'm just a little ahead of things.

"I appreciated it though. The kiss. I mean, that you'd want to kiss me."

"That is a lot of hedging. And, not to brag, but I have a lot of confidence in my kissing ability. People thought kissing me could be a literal hex for years before they stopped. But I completely respect if you're not into me. We can go back to watching the penguins and never talk about this again."

Her smile is warm and genuine. I don't think I'd take someone spurning my advances this well. Not that I'd ever actually advance on anyone. But I remember being very hurt every time someone didn't want to partner up with me in gym.

"I'm not *not* into you! I mean, the kissing was different, and surprising—and, also, I'm ace? But the babbling isn't connected to that. I mean, it's ramped up by me never having to come out in such a relevant situation, but I don't want you to think that all ace people babble in the face of kissing. I'm sure some are as cool as you. Like cool and collected, not cool cool. Though I think you're cool cool too."

I've never wanted a thesaurus so desperately.

"I'm trying really hard not to laugh, because I don't want you to think I'm laughing at you," Sadie says. "It's very sweet that your main concern in this moment is not shaming the ace community by being so adorable."

I'm tempted to ask, "You think I'm adorable?"—but that seems too needy. And I don't *need* confirmation. I just want it.

"We could hold hands. I mean, I wouldn't scream if you did. If you want to."

She slides her hand into mine.

"You can tell me if this is all just an elaborate lie to avoid the curse," she says.

"No! I even have an ace flag pin in the bottom of my backpack—I can get it. It's not on my backpack because it keeps coming undone, and once it stabbed a passing freshman, and I didn't want to cause any bloodshed. Not because I'm not proud."

"Mia, I was kidding. I didn't think you made up a sexuality not to kiss me. Not that that hasn't happened to me before. But I can tell you're an honest person."

"I am. I really am. I've been grounded so many times that I probably could have avoided it if I was a little less dedicated to the truth. Or, you know, just had a better poker face."

"Do you want to get something to eat?" she asks. She's looking at me kindly. I must still look pale. I know that panic babbling drains my face of all color until I look like Satine at the end of *Moulin Rouge*.

"Sure," I say. I decide I'm going to stick to one-word answers for a bit. Safer that way. Plus, it's probably best if I conserve oxygen for my recovery.

We walk to the aquarium café in what I think is comfortable silence. I mean, I'm not comfortable, because there are still so many unanswered questions, and I'm worried my hand is a little too sweaty, which inevitably makes it more sweaty. But I don't get the sense that Sadie is uncomfortable.

I let Sadie get our food, handing her a twenty.

"I'll pay if you pick," I say, hoping this makes me sound smooth and confident, rather than indecisive or just emotionally exhausted.

"No preferences?"

"All of it is overpriced, but all of it is also shaped like animals. There aren't any bad choices," I say.

I watch her walk up to the counter, then consider my feet as I consider my feelings. Or, maybe, more accurately consider my options. My game plan?

Sadie wanted to hold my hand after the shrieking. I would like to hold Sadie's hand more. I wasn't sure if I'd like to kiss Sadie again, but I also felt like maybe she had kissed enough people to hold her over for a while. I knew from talking to Essie and general pop-culture exposure that kissing didn't really work like that for allos, but it must a little, right? Like, yes, I would always be at least a little interested in chocolate cake, but not that interested after eating it every day for a week.

"Penguin chicken tenders," Sadie announces, putting a tray down in front of me, and one in front of her. "It seems a little perverse. Shaping the kind of bird we eat into the kind we never do. Like we're mocking the poor chickens for being less special. Or less cute."

"I hadn't really thought of it like that. The hot honey dipping sauce is really good though."

"So good."

We chew in silence for a few moments. I'm not sure if Sadie was waiting for me to speak, or if she needed time to reflect as well, but eventually I realize letting my thoughts spin is just going to create a giant brain knot (definitely a thing) unless I actually just open my mouth to speak.

"You said your tattoo was part of a good story?" I try. I really want to ask what the song is again, but that seems too demanding. Plus, everyone loves an excuse to tell one of their good stories. Her eyes light up, and I again feel a rush of pride, because I made her feel that way, even if it's just from reminding her of a good memory. If I keep doing that, and stop the shrieking, maybe someday I could be a part of a good memory for her.

"Right, so, what you may or may not know, depending on how bored you've been at a youth orchestra competition in Tampa, is the legal age to get tattooed in the state of Florida is sixteen, and certain parts of our swampiest state have more bargain tattoo parlors than Starbucks."

"I did not know that. Which really is a failing of all their tourism marketing," I say.

"Yes, definitely missing out on an untapped market. Anyway, two of my Academy friends, Julia and Rachel, get very, very sentimental when they drink, which was something we all learned for the first time on *that* trip because they're orchestra nerds who decided to be rebellious by sneaking one hard lemonade each. And in their weepy lemon haze, they called an Uber to bring them to a tattoo parlor called Tough Tatties, swear to god, and convinced each other to get 'BFF,' notated of course, inked on their ankle." Sadie smiles and twirls a piece of her hair around her finger, obviously waiting for me to ask for more.

"And you were too sober to participate?"

"Oh, no. I had had two illegal beverages. But I don't get sentimental when I drink. I get competitive. 'BFF' is three little notes. Hardly seems like a statement. This"—she pulls up a corner of her shirt revealing that the music snakes up from her thigh across her stomach—"is the entire intro to 'You're My Best Friend' by Queen."

"Did they appreciate the gesture?"

"Well, Julia doesn't know who Queen is, because she isn't interested in listening to music written post-1875. And Rachel did eventually, but she passed out shortly after they gave her the 'B,' so most of the trip was comforting her rather than receiving praise for my commitment to the friend group and all of their whims," she says, grinning.

"You don't regret it?"

"No. It takes the pressure off. Getting some kind of musical tattoo always seemed almost inevitable, and now I don't have to think about what the most deep and meaningful option is. Plus, I like Queen," she says, as she rests her hand on top of mine. I try not to hyper-focus on how warm her hand is and how I can feel the piano calluses on her fingers against mine.

"What are your thoughts on dating people who maybe aren't that into kissing and other kissing-related activities?" I can't stop myself from asking, sounding horrifyingly like one of those black-and-white sex ed videos. I really was planning on creating some kind of conversational bridge between tattoos and this, like I'm someone who has talked to people before, but at the moment that seems to be more than I can handle.

"I'm going to need to repeat what I think you said back to you, just for confirmation. Would I mind dating someone who's ace?"

"Yes. I mean, I did ask broadly, but I was asking more about me, specifically," I say. Might as well be direct now.

"Are you asking me out?"

"According to my friends and family, apparently I already did. But I wasn't aware of it at the time. So now I'd like to ask again, aware of it."

"Okay. Well, I was aware of it the first time. But I'd like to go out with you again. Should we maybe plan to hit up a roller coaster? That way if you scream again, no one will stare."

"I appreciate the fact that you're a problem solver," I say, smiling.

"Hey," she says, leaning over to whisper in my ear. "You're not a problem."

———

Two hours after my first date, and I'm still staring at the tiny dolphin-shaped eraser Sadie bought me at the gift shop. I would never tell Brian, and I feel a little guilty even looking at Rosaline now, but this is absolutely my favorite dolphin. I wonder if Sadie feels the same way about the whale whistle I got her. (It seemed musical at the time, but now I'm wondering if its lack of tonality might be an insult to actual musical people.) I consider where to put it. On my desk seems like a natural place, but then I wouldn't be able to see it from my bed. I consider putting it on the pillow next to my head, but that seems too weird. In the end, I pull out the double-sided tape from my very underutilized craft drawer and stick it to the back of my phone case, like a completely ineffective but perfectly adorable Pop-Socket. I stare at it a little bit longer before turning my attention to the now only slightly more interesting side of my phone.

I open ReelLife and check the view count on my first video: 55. I have no idea if that's respectable or even impressive given my follower count of ten (three of which I think might be bots), or maybe just an automatic number the developers give all videos so us under-viewed people don't feel too bad about ourselves. I'm about to close out of it completely when I see a blue notification in my inbox. I open up what I assume is an ad, just because I hate how cluttered apps look with the notification bubble hanging off the side. But it's not.

"Hi, um, HeretoHelp. I had a question I was hoping you could, uh, maybe help with?" I pause the video and stare at the T. rex looking shift-ily at the camera. The T. rex soliciting HeretoHelp's advice. My advice. I click into their account and see this is the only video they've posted, and it's private, meaning my response will be as well. It also means, I realize, that they could be sending a message to every advice account on here, then picking which makes the most sense. But even if that's true, they're still going to hear me out—and this is why I started the account. I want to help. So I'll just have to make sure my advice makes the most sense. I go over to my desk and sit up straight, trying to show this person who cannot see me that I'm giving them my full attention. I unpause the video.

"So, here's the thing. My girlfriend and I are supposed to go on this mega hike this weekend, and she's super excited and has been planning it for months. Every time she brings it up, she says how excited she is to go"—the T. rex hangs its head and lets its arms dangle pathetically. I wonder if they chose this filter because they thought it looked cool and tough, or to maximize the pity anyone listening to their story would feel for them.

"What I haven't mentioned is that I'm afraid of heights. Terrified of heights. Once went on the diving board as a kid, not even the super-high one, looked down, threw up immediately. I don't want to throw up in front of my girlfriend. Or cry. Or scream and refuse to let go of a tree. Should I wait until the day of and tell her I'm sick? Or maybe send a constant stream of articles about how there's a lot of bears in the mountains this time of year? I don't want to disappoint her. But I also don't want to die, you know?"

The video ends with T. rex guy looking sadly at his hands, making me really feel for him. A dinosaur hasn't made me feel so many things since my old babysitter had us watch *The Land Before Time*.

I stack my books once again into my DIY tripod, put on the filters, and hit record.

"Not wanting to die or disappoint anyone are the two biggest driving factors for almost all human decisions. And you probably could get away with playing sick this time. But there are much worse ways for your girl-friend to find out you're afraid of heights. Like midflight in the helicopter she put you in blindfolded for your anniversary. If she cares about you, she'll understand. And if she doesn't, then it's probably best you know that too. As a separate point, if you plan on being together for any extended period of time, the chances go up that she will see you cry or throw up, or both. Make peace with that now, and you can remove a lot of back-ground worry from your day-to-day life." I hit pause, then send. I'm not a competitive person. But in this moment, I still feel confident I just totally beat all the other advice givers and ultimately solved the T. rex's problem. I give my new dolphin eraser a tiny finger high five, which doesn't make any sense (a finger is one of the five, dolphins don't have hands, this dolphin is practically flat) but still leaves me feeling more confident than any confidence-boosting pose ever has.

SIX

"It's our last Halloween," Essie says with all the seriousness and authority of a drill sergeant, her bright purple Doc Martens against Talley's beat-up Toms, their legs outstretched and hands linked, with one pulling the other's torso in between the other's legs, then back again. I know I'm not the best judge, and I know it's one of the official stretches we were all taught in gym freshman year, but it seems so sexual, I can't believe they haven't been told to stop by some of the teachers patrolling the grassy rectangle where seniors are allowed to eat lunch.

"It is not our *last* Halloween," Talley points out. "Unless you know something we don't."

"You know what I mean. The last Halloween we'll all be together," she says, letting go of one of his hands just long enough to steal one of my apple slices.

"Also seems unlikely. I can get to the city for Halloween weekend," I point out, dipping an apple slice in caramel sauce before letting Essie steal it. Talley and Essie were applying to every single college in New York

City, reasoning that being part of the artist community there was more important than any technical "program" in music or theater (I think our guidance counselor might have had a stroke when they explained that), and that they were allowing themselves all the needed post-graduation space as long as they didn't go to the same exact school (but two schools ten minutes apart by subway, totally fine). I would be attending a state school, because . . . money mostly. And if I was going to be tasked with figuring out my entire life over four years, I wanted to do it in commuting range of my family and in three-hour Amtrak range of my best friends.

"It's our last high school Halloween, how about that? It's like neither of you watched that video I sent you on the importance of taking the time to appreciate and celebrate life milestones. But, more to the point—what are we going to be this year?"

While the three of us loved Halloween equally, there was a pretty big fissure in our feelings about costumes. Essie wanted the loudest and most outrageous, Talley wanted the funniest, and I wanted whichever option meant the fewest trips to both Spirit Halloween and Joann Fabrics with both of them.

"What about cats?" I begin.

"We are not being cats, the laziest, most nothing costume—"

"But," I interrupt, "we wear name tags that identify us as the most obscure cats from *Cats*."

"Still feels tired," Talley says.

"But," I start again, because my friends have no faith in me, "we also put dark shadows under our eyes and look otherwise bedraggled, and when anyone asks, we reveal we're actually underpaid extras in the movie of the musical *Cats*. How about that?"

"I like the layers," Talley says appreciatively.

"Okay, I guess that's not technically lazy, because you obviously put in some work on that one, Mia, but still no, because I have the perfect group costume idea," Essie says, detaching herself from Talley and their stretch session and grabbing her phone out of her backpack's front pocket.

I internally sigh. Sometimes I wish Essie would just start a conversation with "This is my great idea and I need you all to listen to it," instead of making us think there's actually room for us in the conversation.

"We're each going as a different iteration of Elton John," she says, holding up her phone and showing us a sea of images of a man in various sequined and feathered outfits. I believe it's important to cultivate at least one wildly, generationally anachronistic interest, the kind that makes elderly neighbors say, "How old are you again?" or, depending on just how far back you're going, might make people believe that maybe you're a vampire. Talley's is this old jazz trumpet player with the best name, Dizzy Gillespie; mine is *Grease* (I just really love Danny's arc—becoming more popular but simultaneously less cool to impress a girl, which is something usually only girls are expected to do in movies); and ever since we watched the movie about Elton John's life on the freshman-year drama field trip, Essie's has been Elton John. I scan the pictures for something that looks like I could throw it together with stuff I find in the costume room and maybe a few things from Target, but there are not many options. This man was just not into minimalism.

"I think I could fit into one of Brian's old lacrosse uniforms from middle school. Is that close enough to the sparkly baseball player?" I ask.

"It is not, but with my bedazzling skills, I'll make it work. Just get it to me ASAP. We've waited way too long on this," Essie says.

Again, I want to point out that as the person with the most opinions on our Halloween costumes, it's kind of on her to kick things off, but again, I keep my mouth shut. Why start drama? It is, after all, our last Halloween.

———

"Okay, everybody. Cratchits in that corner over there, ghosts by the piano, miscellaneous people in the past and present by the mirror, and assorted future people by the sheet music drawers," I call, organizing the cast for our first rehearsal into small-enough groups for manageable get-to-know-you games.

It's a pointless exercise, since everyone already knows everyone except the freshmen, who at least have trauma-bonded together through the audition process, and we'll get to know them in the normal way, through particularly embarrassing line flubs that turn into inside jokes and group mid-rehearsal runs to McDonald's when we learn they like some kind of horrifying food combination like mustard in their McFlurry. But Mr. L likes to check some of the extracurricular boxes, and this is one of them. A box he does not feel the need to check, however, is presiding over this non-dramatic rehearsal moment, meaning I am officially in charge of thirty-four drama kids until the first table read in half an hour. I wait for everyone to shuffle to their respective corners, including Essie, who did land Christmas Yet to Come and has promised to be in charge of the ghost icebreakers so I have one less corner to worry about.

"All right, everybody, so for those of you who don't know, I'm Mia, and I'll be your stage manager this year—" I'm interrupted by light applause and shouts from the two techies, Devan and Julia, who volunteered to help. Their loyalty is sweet, and I make a point of smiling at them in thanks. Devan and Julia have been backstage with me for years, so if anyone knows how hard I worked for the position, it's them. Though I had kind of hoped Essie, who has also witnessed my many set-moving-related bruises and loves loudly making her opinions known, might have clapped just a little. I shrug it off. Her arm is still kind of injured.

"So this is just kind of a get-to-know-you activity so we get a little more comfortable with each other before the table read—"

"What if we're already *very* comfortable with each other?" asks Tiny Tim, a.k.a. sophomore Billy Ralph, grinding against his best friend and current stage father.

"Hopefully this activity gets you to a level of comfort just below that one," I say, which gets a laugh.

"So what we're going to do is go around in a circle—"

"And summon the devil," shouts Teresa M., junior, Ghost of Christmas Past.

"Wrong show, Teresa," I say. "Everyone is going to share their favorite movie."

"What if we feel film is an overrated art form?" asks Kevin, senior, and our Scrooge. I want desperately to mock him and his snobbery, but I know he's actually an incredibly sweet guy who isn't interested in making you feel bad for watching reality TV instead of reading Dickens; he just genuinely believes your life will be better if you do, and he wants you to have a better life.

"Then you can share a favorite book. So everyone goes around once saying their name and favorite, and then the second time, you go around trying to remember what everyone said while making connections. Like, *The Fault in Our Stars* sounds like *Interstellar,* which stars Anne Hathaway, who stars in *Les Misérables,* and the people are all miserable in *World War* Z. Got it?"

There are nods and some scattered *yeah*s. It's an absolute mess of an icebreaker on purpose, just something to get everyone in heated debates about the relative merits of CGI vs. practical effects and whether the right person got cast in a book adaptation. People have very strong opinions about movies, and few things bond you to a stranger faster than finding out you have the same very strong opinion.

"Okay. Learn about each other," I say. I wait for the tentative chatter to reach a legitimate din before I start circling, checking that no one is getting into a physical fight over the best *Star Wars* era or whatever.

Essie is handling her fellow ghosts easily. They're the smallest group, with just four (all the Christmas ghosts plus Jacob Marley), but I figure since they're three upperclassmen plus a sophomore who was only in the spring musical, it would be best to try to connect him to a smaller group. Associated future people are a little rowdy as I pass, but luckily it's out of the joy of common fandom rather than a fandom war. Past and present people are almost completely silent by the time I get there and seem to be seconds away from all pulling out their phones and stopping all possible bonding before I insist they start another round with least favorite films. (It's a risk, but sometimes you have to chance a fight to get some of the less social among us talking.)

"*Finding Nemo* would have been friends with *Blackfish* if it wasn't for corporate greed, which is also what *Wall Street: Money Never Sleeps* is about, and I was a little worried I would never sleep again after I watched

The Babadook," I hear someone finish as I approach the circle. I'm about to congratulate them on incorporating a little social commentary and a little personal info when I recognize her: it's the freshman, now sopho-more, I gave the advice to last spring. The freshman who inspired my first post on HeretoHelp. The freshman I thought was ignoring my advice, but apparently was listening more than I thought.

I'm so pleased I give her, and all of the other Cratchits, a passing thumbs-up before starting my tour of the four corners all over again.

The table read goes by in a blur, as I assume most table reads do when you've heard the play read out loud so many times you've been recorded saying the lines in your sleep on multiple occasions. (Brian found me mut-tering "the founder of the feast indeed" in my sleep so hilarious, he put it in our annual end-of-year family slide show.) Soon it's five, and every-one is packing up, and I'm running after people who left their scripts on their chairs, trying to match fall accessories stuck under table legs to their respective owners, and throwing out granola bar wrappers that always end up half stuck to the risers instead of thrown in the massive trash can I'd left in literally the middle of the room. I'll admit I have a slight amount of residual rage around my edges from cleaning up after indoor litterers when I practically run into the former freshman who took my advice.

"Hey," I say. "I'm glad to see you decided to go out for a play! Are you doing the spirit week committee too?" I ask.

She looks at me with genuine confusion. I hold back a dramatic sigh, not wanting to be rude. So she only absorbed the big-picture advice.

"What I mentioned in the bathroom last year, about not worrying about being in a different extracurricular than your friends?" I prompt. There is absolutely no dawning realization on her face, and I realize suddenly that this girl, either because of the extreme distress she was in or a terrible short-term memory, has absolutely no idea who I am.

"What did make you decide to try out for the show?" I say, pivoting.

"Oh," she says, brightening, obviously relieved she no longer has to tackle whatever memory puzzle I was putting before her. "I saw this Reel-Life video that had some really good advice. Kind of creepy filter though, you know, the void one? You should check it out though. Hold on, I saved it," she says, digging in her pocket for her phone while I try to process the fact that my advice shouted out into the void has reached someone I actually know. And that person actually took the advice. I'm slightly stunned, but the happy kind of stunned, like when a cartoon character just found out they won the big prize and they become a smiling statue. She makes a small noise that I guess means she's found it, tapping her phone a few times before holding it up to my face, and there it is: my own video playing back at me.

"HeretoHelp," I read, trying to sound as if I'm trying out a new word and not my own creation. "Yeah, thanks, I'll check it out." She nods, smiling, then heads out the door.

I remember reading, maybe in some article my mom had left out on the kitchen table, about how scientists deal with the incredible frustration of waiting for results. They know, they just *know*, that playing classical music to plants will help them grow faster, or that adding a certain chemical to a common medication will fight a new disease, or breeding two special types of llamas will produce a super llama who possibly has the power of speech. And most of their work is all hustle, coming up with the theories, then the research that seems to back up the theories, then getting the funding that will allow them to test out the theories. Then they just have to sit back and wait. Sometimes years and years of collecting data before anything like a complete picture can emerge. I realize one instance of someone listening to "void me" instead of "actual me" is what a scientist would call "anecdotal evidence," not the kind they could say is proof of anything.

But I am not a scientist. I am a stage manager. A currently very tired stage manager. A stage manager who is already ready to jump into her next experiment. Or possibly next plot? It has the energy of a plot, I think. Because one person stumbling across my profile is a complete fluke, a combination of fate and probably being in the same zip code, possibly pinging off the same cell phone tower. Holding out hope that the next person I'd like to listen to me is *also* fed my videos is leaving too much up to chance. Giving advice to the unseen masses is nice, and I absolutely felt validated when T. rex guy messaged me a green scaly thumbs-up with the message "Told her—and cried a little. Both went fine." But I also want to help people who I can see, watch the help actually working.

Which means I need to make sure all of drama club is watching HeretoHelp.

Which means I have to talk to Addy.

SEVEN

"Tiniest cousin! How are you?" Addy asks, opening the door to her apartment and waving me in.

"Nearly a legal adult. And one inch taller than the average American woman," I say, giving her a hug before sitting down in one of her many woven hammock chairs hanging from the ceiling.

"Hey, you'll get a new nickname as soon as I get a tinier cousin. Maybe when we're all senior citizens, Kena will start shrinking." Addy disappears into her kitchen and, with almost supernatural speed, reappears holding two martini glasses full of orange soda. Addy's decorating style is what my mother would call eclectic, but I appreciate how almost every decision seems to be made to make every day seem like a special occasion.

"Soooo, I assume you're here to use me, like everyone in the family. Which is fine. I live to serve, for my freelance rate. But wait, let me guess, let me guess. You finally watched *Ferris Bueller*, and you need me to erase some of your absences in the school computer because you've been cutting school? Or you want me to add some, as a cry for attention? Or you got caught up in something in the deep web, and now you need me to show you how to get into the even deeper web?" she asks, raising her eyebrows up and down.

I love Addy so much. The oldest of all my cousins, I didn't really get just how smart she was until high school. I mean, even in elementary school I understood how impressive her résumé was—MIT on a full scholarship at seventeen, working at a giant tech company by her senior year, getting written up in national magazines doing features on young women in STEM. But it was freshman year when one of our other cousins, Carl, first hired her for a "freelance gig" that made me understand that she didn't just know how to do things with computers that her bosses might ask her to do—she knew how to do things with computers her bosses, and basically anyone in charge of an app or a server, definitely *didn't* want her to do. I'm pretty sure she was involved in some kind of hacking (and I'm using hacking with all the nuance and understanding of someone from the '80s, because my tech skills are at the absolute lowest rung of Gen Z knowledge) for a bunch of different activist groups, but she refuses to talk to anyone in the family about it to help us with our "plausible deniability." But she's more than willing to help us with our grand plans, for a small fee.

I have no idea what she helped Carl build, or find, just that he made a fake Yelp review for "Addy's Tech Services" and put it in the cousins' group chat around Thanksgiving that year. He gave her five stars. After that, everyone was coming to her with problems that needed fixing, including Brian with a mystery project last year.

"Can you make my videos on ReelLife reach a certain audience?" I ask, eating the gummy orange slice she had put on the edge of my glass as a garnish.

"Oh, cuz—and I'm saying that in the Shakespearean 'c-u-z' way— you wound me. Audience engagement and growth is beneath me. If you want to give me, like, your half-filled fro-yo loyalty card as payment, I'll send you some links about building your audience. Are you doing like a backstage tour thing for the drama department, because I'll follow you. Ooohh, do you dart out from behind the curtains like the Phantom of the Opera?"

This is not something the Phantom of the Opera does, but I'd never expect someone to know the entire inner workings of the internet *and* the ins and outs of musical theater.

"No, Addy, I'm not. I don't want internet fame or anything. I just want . . ."—I falter for a second before continuing—"my friends to see them." I realize this sounds lame, and even though it's just in front of Addy, I'm embarrassed to admit my ReelLife aspirations are this low.

"Okay, kid, I'm officially confused. Even Grampy knows how to send a link. If you want your friends to see your videos, why don't you just ask them to follow you?"

"For the mystery?" I attempt. I'm not used to being cagey, especially with someone I feel like I can totally be myself with. But I'm worried that if I explain my whole plan to Addy, she'll be able to convince me it's a terrible idea and that the problem can be solved with a heart-to-heart with my friends, or possibly having more confidence. But I am extremely confident that things would be better if my friends would just listen to me. And I've attempted to have heart-to-hearts with Essie and Talley over the years, and there are only so many times you can try to start a serious conversation before you realize you're in a pretty pathetic montage.

"Now you're making me feel like my mom, because that sounds like you're in a crime circle or something. Are you in a crime circle? Or a pyramid scheme? Or in any other unsavory shapes?" She twists her face into comically exaggerated motherly concern. I burst out laughing and decide to trust her with my scheme.

Addy offers me a bag of Goldfish she seems to have fished out from under the couch after I'm done talking. "Okay. I got it. So what you're actually asking me to do is get your void self on their suggested pages, while still keeping your anonymity. Jesus."

"Bad idea?"

"No, anonymity, such a hard word to say." She smiles at me, keeping eye contact as she sips her drink. Addy has learned how to do what I keep hoping Essie and Talley will eventually learn—how to amuse themselves while still paying attention to the person they're talking to.

"So . . . can you do it?" I ask.

"Sure. It's pretty simple, and honestly once just a couple of your theater nerd friends start sharing them among themselves, it'll start happening pretty organically. Even if they don't decide to follow your creepily faceless self."

"But *will* you do it?"

I've never asked Brian what he had Addy do for him, but he did tell me they talked about it for a long time. Actually, what he said was "I totally thought Addy was, like, a computer major, but I asked Mom afterward, and it turns out, she was actually a philosophy major. And after that talk, that makes a lot of sense."

I watch as Addy twirls her deep green hair around her finger, not looking at me, but looking at the suncatcher on her window, which I originally thought was of one dolphin jumping over the other, but looking at it closer, I realize it is two dolphins engaged in an act of oceanic love.

"What's your ultimate plan here?" she finally asks, turning her attention back to me.

"Like you said, if you can kick off the spread, hopefully people will share it and follow it."

"No, I mean, after it spreads. When HeretoHelp becomes all anyone backstage and onstage can talk about, when your friends are ready to make a cult to the brilliance of void person, when everyone is finally following your advice, even though they don't know it's you. Do you confess and bask in the glory? Do you keep it going until graduation, then quietly ride off into the sunset? Do you keep it going for the next twenty years, until they do a podcast about the mysterious identity of HeretoHelp who *has* helped a small community get through college and first marriages and babies? What do you want?"

I think about it for a moment, picking up one of the wire puzzles littering Addy's coffee table and twisting the beaded wires around. I guess when I first created the account, I wanted to see if maybe everyone in drama was right, and my advice wasn't worth listening to. But after the T. rex and then the bathroom freshman proved I was right, and I could have been helping everyone this whole time . . . I want to be helpful. I watch all my friends run around touching power tools and getting into toxic relationships and not checking canned food for signs of botulism, and I know I can help them be happier, safer, if they'd just listen to me. But I know it's not entirely altruistic. I want everyone to know *I* helped them. That they're actually in a better place because of me. I want them to look up from whatever they're doing and look at me for a minute, to appreciate me as their friend, as a person.

"I guess I figure I'll keep it up until the spring musical, and then go for the big reveal at the cast party. Everyone in drama loves . . . dramatic things. Big flourish. Lots of gasps. It'll be like a senior prank, but one I'm doing for validation." And it's true. Not the whole truth—but I'd needed an end game here, too, and I don't really know how to say the rest.

"As someone whose senior prank involved getting every single computer in the school to play 'Cotton Eye Joe' simultaneously, I can tell you everyone does a senior prank for validation." She smiles and looks at me with an expression that seems to say, *I know there might be more that you're not telling me, but I know you know I'm here when you want to explain the rest.* She has a very expressive face.

"What is the going family rate for espionage?" I ask.

Addy laughs. "Honestly, I love that everyone in the family looks at me like I'm the second coming of James Bond at Thanksgiving, but smart devices are absolutely listening to everything we say at all times, so I want to remind the NSA that *I have never engaged in espionage or any other illegal activity.* But for this completely aboveboard little bit of algorithmic manipulation, I'll take fifty dollars."

"That is way less than I thought it would be," I say, getting the cash out of my backpack.

"You think I'm out here up-charging my baby cousins? I only charge for the principle of things, mostly to teach you all, in our glorious and crumbling gig economy, that it's important to get paid for your work." She takes my cash and puts it in a green change purse that looks like a tiny frog.

"So, I hear from multiple reputable sources that you have taken a lover?" Addy says, never one to need smooth or really any conversational transitions at all. I know she's talking like an old-school romance novel just to make me blush, and it works.

"I haven't taken anything, because I believe in personal autonomy—"

"—don't sit there and act like I wasn't the one who gave you your first book of feminist theory, and tell me about her. What's her name?"

"Sadie. And there's a rumor that she has a cursed vagina, but it's not true."

She leans back, looking contemplative. "Wow. High school bullying has gotten super weird."

"You're not going to ask me how I *know* it's not true?"

"Curses aren't real. Well, actually, they are when performed by technopagans, but those only work on machines. She's not a robot, is she?"

"I'm pretty sure she's a human."

"Then I'm confident in your assessment. Fake curse. She handling it okay?"

"I honestly don't think it even bothers her. They basically chased her out of her last school like she was a witch, and she's just, 'Okay, on to the next thing.'"

"She sounds pretty badass. Is she in your theater club? Hiding in the shadows with you or onstage? Oh, you could throw flowers at her feet. Girls love that."

"She's not in drama. She's a pianist. A prodigy actually."

"Ah. So what we need to do is get you a sparkly black gown, so you can lounge on her baby grand as she plays. Or does she know how to play that one song from *Twilight*? She could play that one song from *Twilight*, as a montage of you falling in love seemingly materializes out of thin air,"

Addy says, playing air piano with way more emotion than the dude from *Twilight* did.

"I think we might not be there yet. We've only gone on one date."

"The time for the sparkly black dress will come. But, and I'm putting on my very serious face here, you're comfortable with her? She's chill with you being ace?"

"Yeah. Totally. Definitely," I say, trying to subtly tap my fingers in a mild panic and not succeeding.

"Too many words for a one-word answer. What's up?"

"She's okay with it *now*. But we haven't really talked about what it will mean going forward. *If* things go forward. Because how do you have a conversation about the future without presuming there'll be a future, and that's, you know, presumptuous, and then someone can be, like, 'I would have had a conversation about future things with you if I was planning on having one with you, which I wasn't, how embarrassing for you.'" I say this all in one breath, leaving me slightly winded.

"Kid, listen. I'm not saying I know what it feels like to be exactly where you are, but I can tell you with a hundred percent certainty that people of all sexualities have nervous, walking-on-eggshell conversations about futures neither person are sure will happen with the people they're dating. Everyone is playing this massive game of chicken, only instead of pushing each other in a pool, they're saying stuff like, 'Tara would be a super cute baby name, don't you think?' then watching to see if the other person looks terrified."

"You don't think she'll think I'm conceited for bringing it up?"

"I do not. But honestly, let's say, worst-case scenario, she does—you still want to bring it up, because the stress of not knowing where you

76

stand will wear you down. Give you under-eye circles."

"I already have under-eye circles."

"Yeah, but those are ones from genetics. The purple of your people. Worry turned into insomnia is worse. That will make random people in the supermarket stop you to ask if you're okay. And I know how much you hate making small talk with strangers."

I nod. I do.

"So, you have an awkward-but-no-big-deal conversation with your girlfriend, I'll get the whole John Adams High drama club watching your videos, and by next week your biggest problem will be what to be for Halloween. Has Essie told you what you're going to be yet?"

"We're all going to be different versions of Elton John. But I'm being the version with the least amount of difficulty."

"See?" Addy says, swinging her legs from under her to lie across her coffee table. "It's that kind of naively positive attitude that lets me know you're going to be totally fine."

EIGHT

"This is a date" is what I say when I open the door to let Sadie in. I realize it's customary to say hello to people when you're ushering them into your home, but after the confusion over the last date at the aquarium, I don't want there to be even a minute of this afternoon left to possible misinterpretation. Because "hang out with me at three in the afternoon and we'll probably just watch something on my laptop" doesn't exactly scream "date." Or maybe it does. That's half of what Talley and Essie do when they're alone together. Of course, the other half is sex.

"I know it's a date. That's why I brought these," Sadie says, holding up a bag of gummy roses.

"You got me flowers?"

In my head, I was aiming to say it with affectionate mockery, to show I wasn't taking the gesture too seriously because I'm super cool, and also they're gummy flowers. But it ends up coming out breathless and earnest. I'll admit, if there's a couple thing I've been consistently jealous of, it's the seemingly threefold increase in spontaneous gifts you seem to give in romantic relationships instead of platonic ones. Not because I'm in need of gifts or anything. It just seems really nice to think that at some point when someone wasn't even in the same room as you, they were thinking of you. And there's proof.

"I got you sugar in the shape of flowers, so more practical." Sadie grins. "They're from Sugar Soar—you know it?"

"Sugar . . . Sore . . . ?"

"S-O-A-R . . . I know, I know! It's like they didn't say it out loud, but they have the best fudge. When I was a kid, my parents would always get me gummy roses after a recital." She looks a little wistful, like I imagine an orphan might when talking about past parental gifts.

"Do they . . . not anymore?" I ask tentatively, suddenly realizing all the things I don't know about her tied to this question alone. I'm suddenly concerned she maybe is an orphan, and I've already said something unintentionally braggy about my conspicuously alive parents.

"At some point I guess they decided I was old enough to get real roses. Which did make me feel very sophisticated the first time. But after that, I kind of missed the gummy ones."

I watch Sadie as she kicks off her shoes, then she follows me into the living room. Mom and Dad are still at work, and even though we've never really had the "no guests in your room when we're not home" talk, mostly because I don't think there is a "How to have the talk with your ace teen and, really, do you have to?" wikiHow yet, I figure the living room is a safer bet anyway.

"How's orchestra?" I ask. The revelation of everything I don't know about her has me thinking I should be asking more probing questions, but I haven't had the time to brainstorm and troubleshoot them, so I'm starting with the basics and hoping divine inspiration will strike.

"Discordant," she says, with a straight face for a moment, before letting a smile shine through.

I smile back. She's so funny. Truly cool people don't have to be funny, and someone less confident might even worry that it disturbs the cool vibes, because being funny in front of someone is so close to just asking them to like you, something the truly cool would never do. But obviously Sadie transcends those kinds of rules.

"So, I would have offered that pun either way, but there *is* actually some woodwind drama, unrelated to me, thank god. Biological warfare," she says, her eyebrows rising and falling suggestively.

"Sounds . . . way darker than I would have expected orchestra to be."

"I was chased out of an arts school because of a sex curse."

"Right. So, uh, what exactly happened?"

"So," Sadie says, sitting down on the floor and attempting to tear open the gummy flowers, failing, and then proceeding to rip the bag with her teeth. I can hear Essie in my head say "hot," but I'm just impressed with her resourcefulness.

"Jess, first flute, is apparently in direct competition for the valedictorian spot at St. Mary's with Kelly, first clarinet. Last week Kelly's out with strep. She comes back and will tell anyone who listens that she missed this big chem test the teacher won't let her make up, and that she saw Jess messing with her reeds the week before. And . . ."

"Jess had strep the week before?" I guess.

"She did not. But her little brother did. Which means Kelly is suggesting Jess stole her brother's infected spit and planted it on her reed, possibly with plastic gloves."

"I had no idea St. Mary's was so cutthroat."

"I don't think they are. This is just what happens when you put in too many hours listening to true crime podcasts. You start to see things. Or plot things. No one really thought all those YA murder mysteries would set off a teen murder trend, but I think it has made some people desperate for intrigue." She hands me a gummy rose. "Which is probably fine. I appreciate intrigue." She bites into her own rose. "How are your rehearsals going for *A Christmas Carol?* But remember, no spoilers."

I smile. I always try to be respectful of people's no-spoiler policies, but having one on a two-hundred-year-old piece of literature seems futile. Still, Sadie insists that she's somehow avoided the hundreds of adaptations, and other than knowing there's a mean guy named Scrooge in it, she has no idea how it goes. I'm a little jealous. I would love to know how the story lands when you're not a kid the first time you see it.

"A lot less intrigue than orchestra, apparently. Two breakups, one new couple, one almost breakup, and one tetanus scare when Jacob Marley got cut on his very rusty chains."

"This sounds like a very kinky holiday classic," Sadie says.

The blush creeps up my neck to my ears. I feel like I should be immune to any awkwardness around sex jokes from all the hours spent with Talley and Essie, but I guess there's no real embarrassment vaccine.

"So, what do you want to watch?"

"Have you seen any of *California Girls?*" I ask.

"Nope. But if you can vouch for it, I'm in."

California Girls is a mediocre teen drama at best, something Essie loved in late middle school, which meant we watched it endlessly for multiple summers. Which is how I know the exact episode (season 3, episode 6) when the two stars have a very direct conversation about the next steps in their relationship. And that's my planned segue. I figure it'll make things smoother if there's a natural lead-in to my whole "I'd like to date but possibly only hold hands" conversation.

"Do you mind starting shows kind of in the middle? They always do a surprisingly thorough recap at the start."

"Sure." Sadie leans back against the couch, stretching out her legs. Her socks have individualized toes, which seems like it would be incredibly uncomfortable, but it's super endearing on her. She's so cool and mature and put together, but also she's wearing feet gloves. I want to ask her about them, about her fashion sense in general, but every time I try to formulate a question, it sounds like I'm interviewing her for the school paper. I can hear Talley saying "just be natural," but there's nothing natural about trying to start a relationship. Maybe there is when animal parts of your brain are telling you to stick your tongue down the other person's throat, like all your ancestors have done before you. But otherwise it's just this big extended ask about whether you want to be partners for a group project. The group project being, like, life. I want to grab her hand as we watch TV, to say clearly, we are here together, and also *together* together, but I don't want to risk giving her the wrong idea before we talk. Holding hands while walking seems more natural in a public place, less loaded. You could always just say you didn't want the other person to get lost.

I don't really register anything after one of the titular California girls says, "Previously on . . ." because I'm doing some last-minute editing to my define-the-relationship talk. I know how I'm going to start, that after the DTR discussion on-screen, right when Jessica's face relaxes into obvious relief, I'll say something like "Maybe these California girls are on to something," only not exactly like that, because I'm not a character in a learning English podcast. And then I'll point out all the ways dating me could be totally normal, even beneficial, and possibly pull up that clip from *Pride and Prejudice* where Mr. Darcy has some kind of hand spasm just from brushing Elizabeth's fingers, because even though it's never made any sense to me, I know the internet finds it deeply erotic, so maybe Sadie can start to see hand-holding as practically making out?

"Hey, do you want to go to the winter ball with me?" Sadie says, snapping me out of my planning daze, and for some reason commanding my attention not to her or her question, but the moment playing out on-screen, which is not the DTR, but a more comedic scene involving a dog chase and shockingly large milkshakes.

"The winter ball? That's in two months," I say, with a lot more accusation than I intended, and way more than I deserved to wield, considering that I was about to ask her if she wanted to hang out with me for the foreseeable future.

"You think you'll be sick of me in two months?" she says, looking, to my horror, slightly hurt. I've hurt Sadie's feelings, something a school-wide rumor couldn't manage to do. I backtrack as quickly as possible.

"I was maybe going to ask you out permanently!" I shout, which is alarming for two reasons—volume and the implication I was going to entrap Sadie in some kind of teen marriage. I'm relieved she looks confused rather than scared for her life.

"I mean, like, we could date, like, we could be girlfriends, who also go to the ball. I don't know how they do it at the Academy, but here it's less 'Will you go out on a date' and more 'Will you go steady.' I mean, we wouldn't use those words, because we're not in *Grease*, but it's the same concept, just different, uh, words."

"Are you Greek?" Sadie asks, looking more confused than ever.

"What? Oh, no, not like the country—the movie? It's about the fifties, but from the seventies. They do the hand jive?" I say, before doing a very quick demonstration. It's like I'm playing a game show, and the objective is to give as many details as possible about a movie while still making sure the other person absolutely cannot guess the movie.

"Okay, now I'm a little nervous about bringing you to a dance. Not because there's any shame in what you just did, but because I think if anyone steps into your hand-jive space, you might accidentally kill them," Sadie says, grabbing both my hands. I hope the gesture is both to protect myself and others, and also because she just wants to hold them.

"Very little dancing actually happens at the winter ball," I reassure her. "Mostly it's a lot of picture taking, standing, occasional cupcake eating. And I *would* like to go with you, if the offer's still open."

"It is," she says. "And I saw *Grease* once at summer camp. Does agreeing to go steady with you mean we have to wear matching pleather pants? Because I can buy some, but I'm going to need some advance notice."

I let out a little breath. She's bantering. People don't banter with people they don't like, right?

"There's no required dress code. Well, except, to stay fully dressed. All the time. All the time together, you know?" I should have written this down. I'm teetering on the edge of incomprehensible and bizarrely

84

puritanical, like I'm telling Sadie to cover herself instead of explaining my own disinterest in uncovering myself.

"I know you're ace, Mia, that's cool. I thought we kind of covered this. But if you still need to talk it out or something—"

"I know, but, like, you might say it's fine to be roommates with a competitive opera singer too, because at the start of the school year, you think it's fine, but then it's February and she's running through her scales again, and you just want to go back to your September self and scream 'I made a mistake,'" I say, hoping my metaphor—or maybe my allegory?—landed.

"So, first off, I really appreciate you going with a music-specific metaphor. There are actually these cool sound-muffling masks that singers with roommates use to practice. They make you look like that villain from *Batman*. My friend Vicky literally practices with hers on the bus. But I'm pretty sure what you're actually worried about is whether I'm going to go through some kind of extreme sex withdrawal if we date?"

I nod. A combination of I think better-than-average sex ed and pop culture has taught me that extreme sex withdrawal is both not possible and might also be the reason some teenage boys are so angry.

"Mia, I like you. I like talking with you and holding your hands and learning about the nuances of seventies pop culture with you. And if I feel like my raging teenage hormones are building up to some dangerous level, we can have another conversation. But right now, dating sounds great." Sadie smiles before turning her attention back to the TV, which finally is on the proper scene. After a few moments, she asks: "Did you pick this episode specifically to spark this conversation?" I'm not sure whether that's meant to save me a little embarrassment or because she's riveted by the *California Girls* drama.

"Possibly."

"It sounds very tiring to be you."

"It can be."

She then taps on her shoulder. It takes me a minute to realize she's offering herself as a headrest for my tired self. I'm very happy to accept.

NINE

I wake up on Saturday morning, Halloween, and I can see the blinding sparkle of my bedazzled lacrosse uniform from the other side of the room. Essie truly is a wizard with a BeDazzler. I once suggested she open up an Etsy shop, and she told me she worried it would become so popular, she'd be tempted to give up her Broadway dreams to become a full-time small business owner. I tried to explain to her that having a side hustle could give her some level of financial security as she pursued her dreams, but she ignored me. Actually, she dismissed me with a literal brush-off hand wave like she was the rich manse owner and I was the help in one of those British period dramas she loves. That shut me up for at least two weeks.

My phone buzzes violently on the glass top of my bedside table. I let the notifications roll in until the vibrations shimmy it off and it hits the carpet with a satisfying *thunk* (luckily the case Talley got me for Christmas last year is basically made of bubble wrap).

I go into a backbend off the side of my bed to retrieve it.

Six texts, two from Essie:

I finished the baseball cap, and it's totally up to you if you want to pile your hair into it, so you look closer to Sir John himself, or go with a ponytail, but if you go ponytail, you have to come over half an hour early so I can put the crystals into your hair.

Actually, you should probably come an hour early either way, just in case.

One from Talley:

Essie has been sewing me into my costume for the last hour. Please send help. And bring Kit Kats.

Two from Sadie:

Meeting you at the party at seven, right?

I'll be very impressed if you guess my costume on your first try.

And one from Brian:

> Do you think if I tell the guy from Pizza Palace I'm dressed as a Ditto, they'll give me a free slice?

I give Brian a list of other possibilities for a costume-less costume, promise Talley and Essie I'll be there ASAP, and send a picture of my costume to Sadie to see if she can place mine.

> You're a kid on Jeff Bezos's Little League team? Diamond-encrusted uniforms for the one percent?

> Guess again.

As I'm typing, a notification pops up from ReelLife. Since Addy has done her computer magic, my view count has been going steadily up, and I've heard multiple people reference HeretoHelp during rehearsals. So far I've kept things pretty light in my videos, even linking to advice I've gotten online, to show that I'm not some kind of megalomaniac who only thinks my organic advice is worth listening to—there's the "put a gummy bear on each paragraph as you read to get through a boring homework assignment" recommendation (thanks, sixth-grade-era Tumblr), and one I learned the very, very hard way: always check to make sure your reusable water bottle is all the way closed before you put it in your backpack with your homework, books, and the brand-new graphing calculator your parents were pretty skeptical about you needing anyway.

Plus, I'd thrown out a few relationship advice nuggets, which, I know, what the hell do I know about stuff like that? But just from four years of watching drama, I knew that letting a crush on a friend fester only leads to madness (and by madness, I mean choosing to confess your love onstage, in character, during a really important and *not* romantic moment in *Little Shop of Horrors*); that you really have to decide *before* the morning of Valentine's Day whether you, as a couple, will be celebrating Valentine's Day; and that when figuring out whether you want to stay in a relationship post-graduation, you should probably not ask for a show of hands from your fellow drama kids on whether to stay together or split (or maybe you should if you want a mean, but clear message that you're leaning toward split).

I open the app to see I have a direct message. I assume it's from a bot or Addy, since no one has messaged me directly since T. rex guy besides Addy. Addy's messages always just involve a lot of winking and quotes from Sherlock Holmes ("The game is afoot" and her throwing a lot of shoes at her camera, for example).

When I open it up, a video plays of someone using one of the seasonal filters, their head gone (but an outline still kind of moving as they talk), and their hand holding up a jack-o'-lantern. They talk in a whisper-echo voice I believe is the witch filter. I appreciate their commitment to spooky vibes.

"So, I don't normally ask people or, I mean, strangers for advice. But this is something I just don't . . . I don't know. I don't really want to talk to anyone I *do* know, you know? Fuck, I sound so stupid. You're probably trying to figure out how to give advice to a stupid person right now. Anyway, so, I just found out I got into this show, and it's a pretty big deal. I mean, it's regional, which is only, like, three steps below Broadway. I didn't tell anyone, like, *anyone* about auditioning because I knew it would become a thing, and why make it a thing when I wasn't going to get the part? But I got it. I got the part. And if I take it, it means I'm going to miss some stuff. Like my last high school musical. Whole pieces of my senior year. Fuck, les frites ne sont pas si françaises."

I gasp. Audibly, dramatically gasp and pause the video. It's Essie. The headless horseman is Essie, asking void me for advice with something she couldn't even be bothered to tell me about in real life. I know because of the French—"les frites ne sont pas si françaises" means "French fries aren't really French," and it's her filler sentence, the one she always uses on her French exams when she doesn't know the answer. Most people in drama use their filler sentences in real life as a joke, like you don't know what to say so you answer someone, "Mi tortuga es enfuego." ("My turtle is on fire," if you need the translation.)

But Essie, though she'd only ever admit this to Talley and me, feels more confident when she speaks French, so she'll often throw it into conversation, under her breath, when she's feeling stressed. And right now, she's stressed out because she went for the open call she promised Talley she wouldn't go to. It was posted online and forwarded to her by one of her theater camp friends, a production of *Spring Awakening* happening at our regional house. It would mean no spring musical at school, missing just about anything happening on the weekends from January through April, and there was even a production date on prom. She'd floated the idea to us faux casually one night in September, and before I got a chance to tell her to go for it, Talley was asking her how she could even consider giving up the second half of their senior year together; all these places where memories should go just big holes, with voice memos and texts trying to fill in the gaps. And I wasn't going to give her advice that would contradict Talley's, that would probably lead to a fight, that could possibly lead to a breakup, that would inevitably lead to me having to choose sides, which would result in my almost certain complete mental and emotional collapse.

She'd promised us, though mostly Talley, that she wasn't going to do it.

I know I should probably be mad at her lying, at the very least be mad at the lying on behalf of Talley, and it *is* super shitty of her to go behind his back. Still, I'm mostly proud of her. She's been saying it's time for the next step in her career for years. Even thinking it seems disloyal, but I had been starting to wonder if, even with all her talent, she might just put off auditioning forever, until acting became some distant dream she had had when she was young. I unpause the video.

"So I guess what I'm asking is should I take the role? It's a huge opportunity, and I want to, I really, really want to, but I don't want to hurt the people I'd be sort of leaving behind. I mean, not leaving behind really, I'd still see them at school, but . . . that's what it will feel like to me, so I think it would have to feel like that to them. What do I do?"

I realize I would have known it was Essie even without the French. The way she tips her head to the side while twirling a piece of hair when she finishes her thought is something she's been doing since seventh grade. And not even the voice modulator can hide the weird vocal dips she'll sometimes adopt to make triple sure she's not doing upspeak.

I'm also certain, in this moment, that whatever HeretoHelp advises, Essie will do. Not because my wisdom will be so apparent, but because she obviously wants to put this decision in someone else's hands. Someone's totally unbiased hands. I could tell her to pass it up and be responsible for making sure she's with us through all the senior lasts that I know she cares about too. It wouldn't be completely selfish. Sure, she might have a twinge of regret when she sees the posters go up for opening night, but that wouldn't matter when she requested "The Hampster Dance" for the fifth time at prom. I could make that happen.

I know that's what Talley wants. For her to turn down the part and spend their senior year together. But I also think now that the part isn't a hypothetical, now that Essie actually landed it, that any anger he has will be overshadowed by pride, by happiness for her. Because Talley is a good boyfriend and a good guy, and that's the kind of reaction you'd expect from a good guy, right? I open up the response option, put on the void filter, and hit record.

"To the headless horseman this Halloween. Losing any time with your friends is going to suck. I'm not going to say it won't. You're going to see pictures of moments where you can sense the vague outline of where you were supposed to be, and it's going to really, really sting. Even if they caption it 'Wish you were here.' But you went to that audition for a reason. You knew you're ready to be on a stage bigger than the one at your high school. I think there's going to be a part of you that regrets whatever decision you make, just a little bit. But I also think choosing to turn down that part is what you'll regret even more."

I pause for a moment, my finger hovering over the send button, but I think that's more because I feel the gravity of the situation, not that I'm really second-guessing my advice. I know what's best for Essie. And that's what I want for her. Regret is dangerous. I've seen it in the faces of some teachers talking about our college plans, how what they didn't do haunts them. I won't let Essie be haunted. I hit send, toss my phone onto the end of my bed, and start getting ready for the party. Something that no one but me knows is really one of our last lasts.

TEN

It's not even 9 p.m., and someone is throwing up in the Jemsons' garage. Specifically, in one of the giant Rubbermaid containers that holds all the roller skates and tennis rackets they've collected over decades. I don't envy the cleaning job Rebecca will have tomorrow morning, but you have to know when you host basically the entire performing arts department on Halloween, there's going to be some level of destruction. We collectively have a lot of feelings and a need to express those feelings, and it's not hard to convince yourself a great way to ease that expression is downing one of each color of whatever barely alcoholic drink one of the older-looking seniors has managed to bring. I assume that if my vaguely green-tinged peers had actually talked out some of those feelings, there'd be less vomit in Rebecca's sister's Barbie helmet, but I have bigger problems, because this is basically the first time Essie, Talley, and Sadie have all hung out together. Which means I need to be on high alert for anything that could even possibly become a conflict.

Essie is eyeing the puker warily over the top of her giant bejeweled sunglasses, radiating "no one better even think of messing with my costume" energy. Her Elton John homage is pretty spectacular, complete with bejeweled swimming cap and giant jewel-colored feathers sprouting from the back of her jacket that almost touch the ceiling.

Talley, though very pleased in all our group photos, looks fairly uncomfortable in his giant Donald Duck suit at the moment, because even though Essie took care to tailor it perfectly to his measurements, it's still not easy to sit in, and nearly impossible to remove for bathroom runs. The two of them are leaning on each other both in affection and I think to counterbalance the sheer weight of their costumes. I thought it would be more difficult than it was not to say anything to Essie about the video or the audition while we got ready, but everything was so chaotic with last-minute additions being sewed there and glued here, I barely had time to think about it. But now, after eating several pounds of Nerds (and Nerds Rope), with only the sound of retching to interrupt the playlist of creaky floorboards (Rebecca's parents had told us to keep things down after we had scream-sang "Defying Gravity," and her solution was to play only Halloween effects in the public domain), knowing that I knew but Essie didn't know that I knew was weighing on me again. I was about to casually bring up *Spring Awakening*, or possibly just seasons in general, to really ease into things, when Sadie came back from getting us all some nonalcoholic drinks (because of strict parent, not wanting to mess with her voice, thinks it tastes like fire, and a general law-abiding nature).

"So, did you guess yet?" Sadie asks. I stare at her, knowing Talley and Essie were also playing her costume mystery game. She looks absolutely stunning, in a black floor-length gown I'm pretty sure she had to wear for recitals at the Academy. She isn't quite in the right outfit to take the stage at junior orchestra, though, because her wrists are encircled in giant orange-red sponge-looking bracelets, and the same spongy things are sticking out of the two space buns she had pulled her hair into. She's also wearing drop earrings made up of silver wires dotted with tiny shells.

"You're Aquaman, but fancy and gender bent?" Talley suggests, bracing himself to sit down with his arms in front of him like he's about to attempt a backflip, then quickly and violently sinking to the ground, very narrowly missing a seemingly sticky purplish puddle.

"Nope. Though I really hope somewhere, someone is wearing that," Sadie says with a contemplative grin, as if imagining a whole room of gender-nonconforming DC Comics people.

"You're a student at the Academy, but someone wants your chair, or whatever, so they've poisoned you with a thing that makes you break out in . . . orange stuff," I vote.

"I love that you already understand the Academy so thoroughly, Mia. But no."

Essie looks Sadie up and down, almost in a bored way. She'd been true to her word in spreading the very pointed message that curses were stupid, and we weren't going to be bullies like the Academy kids (and adults). But she still always seemed to be looking at Sadie like she wished she would just . . . go somewhere else. Which was unfortunate, because we were often standing in the same place, and I always wished Sadie would be right next to me, close enough that we might occasionally tap elbows.

"You're choral coral," Essie says.

"She got it," Sadie says, looking way more excited about Essie's victory than Essie does.

"I do pun costumes every year," Sadie explains.

"Cool," Essie says flatly. Which isn't a bitchy thing to say, exactly, but something about her tone and general dead-eyed expression makes me want to call her out on it. But calling her out would make Essie defensive, which would make Talley protective, which could end in both of them ganging up on me, and I'm not quite sure what would be worse, if Sadie came to my defense, gallantly, or if she didn't.

"So," Sadie says, with a more forced smile now, apparently trying to steamroll over Essie's bad mood, an impulse I applaud, even if I doubt it will work. "First drama party. The music choices are . . . interesting. Solid food selection. Are you guys going to play that zip-zap-zop game from camp or, like, monologue at each other?"

"Well, first off, if we monologued at each other, it would be a dialogue," Essie says.

"Yeah, I know. It was a joke. I didn't think you were actually going to stage a production in this garage or anything." Sadie laughs.

I mean to groan internally, but a little comes out loud. Because that's exactly what was going to happen.

"So, uh, like three Christmases ago, Kevin—you know, the guy playing Scrooge—went to New York with his older brother, and they saw one of those Drunk Shakespeare shows, where the cast keeps drinking and still keeping up with the plot and the couplets even as they're getting, you know, compromised. So we started doing that at parties."

"Drunk Shakespeare?" Sadie asks.

"Actually, no one here is really that into Shakespeare—" Talley starts.

"—because they have no culture—" interjects Essie, before I cut her off.

"You fell asleep during *Macbeth*, Essie. Anyway, the people who actually drink try to put together a semi-stable version of whatever show we're doing at the time. So tonight, very unseasonably, you're going to be treated to *A Christmas Carol*," I say, with a little curtsy, like I'm already presenting it. "And honestly, some of them are so distant from the source material, you still might avoid most spoilers."

"Wow, you guys are always working. I promise no one is pulling out their clarinets at Academy parties. Well, there was one time when the Jasons got practically blackout drunk and used them for a sword fight, but that doesn't really count."

"We're dedicated to our craft," Essie says, in a self-serious way I don't think I've heard her use since she was running for student council in eighth grade. I attempt to give her a look that says "Chill, please, it's important to me that you like each other, or that you like me enough to pretend that you like each other," but as soon as we lock eyes, she gives a little shrug and turns her attention back to lightly glaring at Sadie. And I know that she didn't literally say "Fuck you and your feelings," but it's hard not to take it that way. I shrug too, not in retaliation, but in an attempt to shake off the feeling Essie is actively rooting against me and Sadie.

"I'm not sure 'Drunk Christmas Carol' is something you can put on your college app résumé," I point out.

"Not everything is about college, Mia. Some of us are looking past that. Into our real futures."

I know Essie has big actor dreams, but it's still weird to know someone who can see past the next four years.

"Okay, E. You going to tell us we're all in *The Matrix* too?" Talley says from the floor, referencing his older brother's favorite movie that I've fallen asleep during twice, but I know involves a lot of fighting and questioning your own perception of reality; two things I'd like to avoid.

"Whatever. I want to play Scrooge, so I'm going to go do a few shots with Rebecca. You coming?" Essie looks at Talley and me, but not at Sadie. I wouldn't have actually thought that was possible, but it's like lasers are coming out of her eyes to say, very clearly, that her invitation does not extend to my girlfriend. "Essie, what the hell?" is caught in my throat. It's what I want to say but can't, because I don't talk to people like that. I definitely don't talk to my best friend like that. So I just say, "Sadie and I will chill here till curtain. Break a leg."

Essie's eyes narrow in annoyance, and I worry she's about to say something even more cutting, but she just bends over to help Talley up, and the two of them walk over to the table covered in tiny red plastic shot glasses and bright orange plastic spider rings.

"Any idea what I did to make your friend hate me?" Sadie says, remarkably casually, like people hate her all the time. Which is ridiculous, because I don't know why anyone wouldn't like her, and if you knew people hated you, how could you just walk around without the knowledge crushing you into a sad human pancake?

"She doesn't hate you," I hurry to explain. "She's just stressed out. You know, senior year, she has a bunch of college auditions coming up. She never read that book I got her on releasing stress before you start directing it outward . . ." I say the last bit as a joke, but I did think the book could have helped her. And maybe I kind of wish she'd even tried to lie about reading it when I saw it in a spring-cleaning donate pile.

"Sure. I get that. But she's directing her stress rage *just* at me. I'm assuming she just doesn't like to share you, but I just wanted to double-check I hadn't disrespected the ghost of Sondheim or something I should apologize for."

"Essie's more of a Lin-Manuel Miranda fan, but I don't think she has a problem with sharing me," I point out. "I mean, we share Talley, and she shares Talley with me, since middle school." I thought the dynamic of our friendship was pretty obvious, but I guess nothing is as obvious to an outsider as it is to someone inside a relationship.

"No, I get it. You're a third wheel, but on a tricycle. You are some kind of unpaid, full-time mediator for their relationship. And she's worried being with me might make you realize you might want to spend more of your time doing . . . not that."

I'm momentarily too stunned to speak. Because that's not what I do. I mean, sure, sometimes I'm the peacemaker between the two of them, but that's because *I* need peace. They'd be fine with living in some kind of tense standoff for months at a time, while my life expectancy took a nose dive (stress chips away at it, according to multiple studies I stress-read a few years ago). And it's not like I don't have other friends. I'm friends with practically everyone in this garage, to one degree or another. It's not like Sadie was the first person cutting into my Talley and Essie time.

Maybe the first person taking up such large chunks on her own, but that shouldn't really matter to them. Should it?

"Hey, hey, I did not mean to push you toward some kind of painful revelation during 'Monster Mash,'" Sadie says gently. "I'm not judging, or anything. If this is what works for you, if this is making you happy, I will just deal with the death glares. Maybe I'll get cool sunglasses to help deflect them. Do you think Essie would bedazzle them for me if I offer to pay her? I could confuse her into liking me, through capitalism."

"Essie definitely likes you. She was just telling me yesterday she was happy I was with someone," I say.

She had said that. I was being completely honest, as I always try to be, as long as that honesty won't piss someone off. Of course, what she said after that was "Now you can get through all the stages of figuring out a relationship the first time, so next time it will be so much easier."

At the time, I thought that was just Essie being practical. I mean, statistically, the first person you start dating in high school is not the person you end up being buried next to. But maybe referencing the end of our relationship so close to its start was a little meaner than I'd like to admit. Maybe Essie was always a little meaner than I'd like to admit. But as long as I'm aware of that, I feel like accepting said meanness is a choice I'm making, not just something that's happening to me.

"Well, I'm dating *you*, not Essie. We'll either grow on each other, or we'll get better at hiding our discomfort at parties. Which, my mother has told me, is an important skill to develop anyway. Do you want to dance?" She tacks the request on naturally, like her brain has happily moved on to the next subject, not like she's desperately trying to distract herself from potential months or years of future conflict.

"I'm afraid my only move really is the hand jive," I say, looking apologetically at my hands.

"It's the same time signature, just slowed down a lot. It'll work," Sadie says, guiding me toward the dance floor with one hand while very slowly hand-jiving with the other. It showcases more coordination than I've ever possessed. What can I do but, much less gracefully, follow her lead?

"Five minutes to places!" calls Toby, a freshman techie. I'm off for the night, and, really, the call is more for the audience than the thoroughly tipsy players, who are already positioned in front of the Jemsons' garage door, the de facto stage.

Some people have flipped over storage buckets (hopefully the ones without puke in them) to use as chairs along with a handful of soccer mom chairs and foldable beach ones. Sadie motions me over to what I realize is three old dog beds stacked on top of each other (Porkchop, their one and only golden retriever, is alive and well, just in the habit of rejecting beds he believes are beneath him), and we both sink into the fur-covered tower.

"It was the best of times, it was the worst of times," Essie announces, holding out her arm toward the audience.

"Wrong show," calls a dude I don't recognize, obviously someone's non–performing arts date.

"That was a *test*," Essie says, narrowing her eyes and crossing to the lawn mower (downstage left).

"Marley was dead to begin with," she declares, in an impressive ghost story voice, her phone, with the flashlight on, tipped toward her chin.

"All right, who killed me? Was it the people I evicted, the people I let starve, the people I convinced to join my pyramid scheme?" calls Nate as Jacob Marley, who is dedicated enough to have brought his chains to the party and has draped them over the Spider-Man suit he's worn for the last three Halloweens.

"No, Jacob. It was I, the most deadly killer of all . . . a minor cut before penicillin was invented," someone calls from behind something, their voice more muffled than spooky.

"Jacob, speak comfort to me. I'm on my knees!" Essie says. She is not actually on her knees, as that would mess up her costume, but she does look appropriately pleading.

"Okay. Um, hell isn't dull. Always a lot going on. I'm meeting new people every day—"

"That's not comforting! What can I do to avoid this fate?"

"What if you donate your entire net worth, while you're alive? And, in general, don't be a dick to people?"

"Well, that sounds pretty straightforward. But . . . as you know, I've always been suspicious of things that are too straightforward. Could I get a second opinion? And possibly a third and fourth?"

"But there are only three ghosts," Jenna, one of the Cratchit kids, says in what she thinks is a whisper.

"Four, including Marley," someone from the audience yells. Essie glares again. Even though this is really just a very elaborate (and deeply dorky) party game, it's still technically a performance, which means Essie is taking it seriously.

"Sure, why not. Expect the first ghost in, like, a hot second," Nate says, before lumbering out back into the audience, where his boyfriend Robbie immediately starts untangling the chains and rubbing his shoulders.

"I am the Ghost of Christmas Past! I know all the lines from all the old Christmas movies! Go ahead, quiz me! The black-and-white ones too!" Isabelle decrees, sweeping on the stage in her impressive Marie Antoinette (the Sofia Coppola version) dress.

"We'll do that later," Essie says. "Spirit, will you show me a simpler time, a time when I remembered the true spirit of Christmas?"

"I, uh, fuck, Essie, I don't, it's not even that I'm drunk, I'm just not in an improv place right now. Can we just skip me?" Isabelle asks. Essie nods and shoos her off to the corner.

"You know," Sadie whispers in my ear. "Any version I see after this one is really going to be a letdown."

"That's a good point. Come on," I say, motioning for her to follow me out of the garage just as George, Ghost of Christmas Present, screams, "No, Scrooge, I swear to god you *can* hollow out a candy cane with your tongue and use it as a straw, I saw it on ReelLife. It makes everything taste like Christmas!"

I pull Sadie around the side of the house, and all of a sudden she's grabbing my waist and I'm in the air, spun half around and gently set back down on the grass.

"What—"

"Sorry, you were about to step in dog poop," she says.

"And your solution was to suddenly turn us into ballroom dancers?"

"Well, I'm already a ballroom dancer, so it was only sudden for you."

"Seriously?"

"Yeah. My mom thought I was sitting too much as a kid, always on the piano bench, and instead of signing me up for travel soccer and moving the needle a little closer to normal childhood, she just doubled down on weirdness. Which I really appreciate. I'm now ready to impress at any dance and, if my dad's spy movies are right, get almost any information out of a bad guy during a tango."

I lean back against the vinyl boards of the house, the cold condensation creeping through the not terribly thick fabric of my costume.

"This is where we'd kiss, in a movie," I say, before thinking about the possible implications of what I'm saying. Because I meant it as an observation, a kind of site-specific Snapple fact. But I know it might sound like I'm suggesting something.

"I have made out behind many garages. Never with this much coral on my head though," Sadie says. We both stay turned out toward the moon, rather than turn to look at each other. I think Sadie is doing it to give me space. I'm not sure why I'm doing it.

"We could kiss a little, if you want?"

"Is that something you want?"

This is an excellent question. I don't *not* want it. I'm not repulsed by the idea. And I'm curious, in an anthropologic way, what kissing—not a single gentle kiss, but actual continuous making out—is actually like. It's kind of like how I felt when my cousin took me to her youth group a few years ago. I mean, did I want to learn about Jesus and Jesus-adjacent things? No. But I had spent so much of my life hearing references to church, I did want to see what all the fuss was about.

"I think there could be worse ways to spend Halloween."

"I don't want to pressure you."

"I'm the one bringing it up."

"Right. But I just want to make sure you're not bringing it up because you think it's something I want."

"Don't you want to?"

It strikes me that even though we settled the dating thing, I probably shouldn't assume Sadie wants to make out with me under all circumstances. Maybe the lacrosse uniform weirds her out, or the smell of vomit is a mood killer, or over the course of our as-of-yet-short relationship she's had the dawning realization that this whole asexual thing is perfect, because even though I've charmed her with my dazzling personality, there's still the slight problem of my face.

She turns then. It seems like a cliché to think she looks beautiful in the moonlight, but the truth is she looks beautiful in every lighting I've seen her in so far—this is just the newest.

"Mia, what I'd like to do, specifically, is pin your arms above your head against this house, lean into you very gently, then kiss you until both our lips are chapped."

She's looking at me so intensely, and all I want to tell her is that it's so sweet that she was thinking enough about kissing me that she broke it into steps, but Essie has told me more than once that, other than the very important step of establishing consent (or, just as important, revoking it), sometimes overtalking can kill a mood. And she seems so excited about this whole thing, I don't want to ruin it for her, so I just say, "Sounds like a good plan to me."

And then suddenly my arms are above my head, and I'm struck by how much taller Sadie is than me, and stronger. When she leans in, I can smell her perfume, or maybe her body wash—strawberries and cream.

Her lips are soft, and as she starts to speed up and slow down, it occurs to me that she might be very good at this, and it's kind of a shame that her skill is being wasted on me. It's nice though. Nice to be certain, more than I think I've ever been in my life, that I'm receiving someone's full attention. Nice that as she kisses me with more intensity, I think it's safe to think that there's something about me that's making her want more. It's nice to be so close to her, to think that if we're this mashed together, physically, it must mean we're really close. Or getting close. My arms are starting to get a little tingly from lack of blood flow, and I know there's no polite way to point this out, so I am relieved when she lowers them down, kissing my neck gently as she does. I wonder if I'll get a hickey. I think we might be too old for that kind of misstep, or maybe the whole thing is a little old-fashioned. (I feel like I've seen them referenced in old movies more than new ones, but what could possibly account for that, unless we were evolving to have thicker neck skin?)

"Was that okay?" she whispers, searching my face. I hope she doesn't find what's underneath, that I spent that whole time thinking, not feeling, as she was, as I'm sure she'd like to think I was.

"It was nice," I say. I hope that will strike her as a neutral adjective, not an accusation. And it was nice. Nice to be seen, nice to be connected, nice to be wanted. And I get that we wanted slightly different things from the moment, but as long as we both got a collection of nice things from it, that should be enough, right?

She's about to say something when the play spills out from the garage, Essie's voice booming and pissed.

"Jesus Christ, Richie, I do not need to debate with you whether it's still Halloween because we should go by the ancient Celtic calendar, just say, 'Why, it's Christmas Day.'"

Sadie's face scrunches a bit with a valiant effort not to laugh.

"Isn't Scrooge supposed to be nice in the end?" she asks.

"Essie has never been opposed to taking liberties with a classic."

"Do you want to go back in and watch the end?" she asks.

This is my last drama Halloween party. But it's also my first with Sadie. I reach for her hand and put my fingers through hers.

"Let's stay out here a little longer."

ELEVEN

"Essie done pointing yet?" Talley asks as he slides down next to me on the wall outside the drama room. Technically, I had been excused from this particular run-through of the show to do outreach and promotion, which means calling our town's five local restaurants to double-check if they're still chill with us leaving flyers on their community board, then sending all the techies with driver's licenses out to canvas. Normally, the week before tech week would mean I was writing down blocking, or at least staying on book so actors could call out "line." But since Mr. L had blocked our *Christmas Carol* since before we were born, and if someone happened to space on a line they normally had the gist and everyone would just roll with it, I instead had time to put together my very low-stress college applications. I almost feel guilty how unworried I am about the common app on my laptop—so many people around me are freaking out about their college auditions, trying to get the right balance of safety schools and reaches, trying to shoehorn an extracurricular in at the last minute (we did not need thirteen seniors I barely recognized for our set

110

repainting session last week), and I'm just writing 250 words on my favorite book and sending in my perfectly respectable grades and SAT scores to two state schools that had both accepted Miles Radcliff, a double super senior a few years back who became somewhat of a legend for accidentally showing up for the first day of school the fall after he graduated, according to him, out of muscle memory.

"Essie has twenty more minutes of pointing at least," I tell Talley, not looking up until he slowly begins to close my computer.

"It's rude to ignore your friends," he says, as I stare at my now-closed computer.

"It could be argued that it's even ruder to interrupt a friend as she's taking a momentous step toward her future."

"You're applying to North Connecticut State. Not momentous."

"You are a college snob, and I'm sending you an article on the merits of state schools right now."

"I have nothing against state schools. I just mean, for you, it's not momentous."

I look at him, to see he's not looking at me but is instead scribbling something in his lyrics journal. Because apparently he's allowed to multitask while we talk.

"What do you mean, for me?"

"You know."

"I do not know." I want to close his journal or take the pen out of his hand, which should be okay, because he just established that's a completely fine way to get someone's attention. But it still feels too confrontational. And my mild annoyance isn't worth making him legitimately annoyed. Probably.

"I mean I don't really see a future you, you know?"

I have no idea what to say to that, so I just kind of gape at him until he finally looks at me.

"Not, like—I just mean you don't have any plans."

"I plan to go to college. That's a whole four years' worth of a plan."

"Right, but to study what?"

"Many different things. Talley, are you saying every undecided freshman should be killed in some kind of ritual sacrifice? Because that's harsh."

He looks up at the ceiling, not annoyed but pensive. Like he's trying to figure out how to clarify that my future is full of endless possibilities, and something so wide and open is maybe too hard for him to conceptualize. That it was definitely a failure of his imagination that made him look at me and say I didn't have a future.

"I guess I just can't picture you as Mia the . . . You know?"

"It's true, I don't think I'm going to be a professional wrestler . . ."

"You're Mia, and you're an amazing human being. And friend. But when I try to picture you having a job or, like, a thing, I can't."

"I have things, Talley."

"Right. No, I know you do," he says, but he's already scribbling something else. I have a ReelLife channel with over a thousand subscribers, I want to say. But it's not even about that. I've never cared that I wasn't the art kid or the sports kid, or even when I realized I'm a theater kid with no plans for becoming a theater adult, at least not in an official way. But Talley thinking that means I'm less of a person, somehow, makes my eyes burn.

"Hey, did you get my new lyrics? I shared the doc the other night."

"Yup."

Though a futureless person seems like a poor choice for a beta reader. I almost say it out loud before I bite my tongue.

"You can comment right on them, I have a duplicate file."

I know things about your girlfriend you don't know. I take a deep breath.

"Okay, my butt's asleep. Want to wait for Essie with me at I Scream!?"

I can't leave right now. I have a thing, a THING, a title and a job and three new messages in ReelLife from people who think I might have the answers. And I do have the answers. All Talley ever had was questions—what do you think of these lyrics, does this song work here, should I get a faux-hawk? Maybe I don't have one consuming passion, but at least I have enough confidence to pick out an outfit for a random Tuesday without getting a friend to weigh in.

I shouldn't have such mean thoughts about Talley. I shouldn't. I will Talley to ask me what's wrong as I take a deep breath, and hiss it out through my teeth, picturing the anger leaking out of me, as invisible as air. It is not the long exhale of someone who is completely okay, and a best friend should probably notice that.

But he's already walking toward the door.

"I have to stay to the end of practice. I'll tell Essie you're waiting for her at I Scream!" I offer. Even though he's more than capable of texting her himself. Even though it's possible I didn't let all my anger toward him leak out, and I'm tempted to just forget to tell Essie.

"Cool. Check out those lyrics tonight, yeah? You're the best," he says, before opening one of the three-ton exit doors with a dramatic slam and walking into the parking lot.

I look after him for a moment before opening ReelLife. Which I suppose I should be a little more careful about doing in a public place, but I put in my headphones and figure I'll be able to close it before anyone gets close enough to really make out what was playing on the screen.

I don't go to my inbox right away. Because that would make this into something it's not. I opened the app because I'm feeling a lot of things, and scrolling through video clips is the best way I can think of to feel nothing. Or maybe think nothing. Or maybe crowd my brain with so many images and sounds, none of my actual thoughts would actually fit. I did not open the app to show Talley. That would be futile. You can't throw a retort at someone once they've already left. I finally go to my inbox that's blinking with three messages. I always get a little thrill when I see the notification. So far I've steered one freshman toward some websites that might help her with her fears of the dark and hopefully, hopefully convinced someone I didn't recognize that asking out two people at the same time while figuring one will say no is a really, really bad plan. I scan the messages. Two, based on the usernames alone, are definitely not human. I click into the one sent by BroadwayBaby99. A koala is staring back at me, and even though it's one of the clunkier filters, I can still tell the person behind the marsupial is pretty uncomfortable.

"I guess I just wonder if you have any . . . tips? Or maybe insight. Things are just a lot right now. Maybe it would be okay if rehearsal and soccer practice weren't back-to-back. Every other day would be fine, but I just feel like I can't catch my breath. And that's not even fitting in studying, and maybe seeing my boyfriend for more than five minutes, when he'll tell me I look tired, and, like, no shit, and I hate that that pisses me off, because that's what pisses my mom off, when my dad says she looks tired, so now I'm this overtired seventeen-year-old who's already her mom, which I thought wasn't supposed to happen until you were like twenty-five. So. Help?"

If drama's entire population had been a little sportier, this might be harder, but there's exactly one person in *A Christmas Carol* who is also on the soccer team: Jessica, a junior I always think of as the star of morning announcements, because during the daily roundup of the administration bragging about things we did that they really have no claim to, Jessica's name pops up the most. She's always getting a statewide sportsmanship award for being both really good at kicking and really good at interpersonal skills, or getting some kind of gift certificate from the mayor for taking all the standardized tests in alphabetical order and acing every single one. She's also an amazing singer and genuinely really nice, and also had to be woken up backstage during a performance right before her cue multiple times. One of my stage manager predecessors had started calling her narcolepsy jock, apparently with so much consistency a well-meaning sophomore had forwarded her links to a therapy that had apparently worked for her cousin, who really did have narcolepsy. It *was* stressful having her in the cast, though, because she made me nervous about having someone show up to talk to an English townsperson who wasn't actually there. But it's not like she was on her phone or had headphones on or something, and it felt too harsh to call someone out for just getting some sleep. I always thought a little less of teachers who turned waking up a sleeping student into some kind of prank video, dropping books on their desk after making sure the whole class was ready to see them start and sputter. I mean, their body had told them, "I'm out, recharging right the hell now, on an uncomfortable metal chair in a position that will give you back problems before you can legally vote." Maybe they need it. But if being overscheduled is what's making Jessica pass out on the costume couch, maybe what she needs is just a better actual scheduler. I know I've found more pockets of time after my mom got me a fancy color-coded planner and Essie started sending me bullet journal explainer videos. I pull up links to a few of my favorites to put in the caption, then open my notes app to draft the video I'll record as soon as I get home.

Feeling like you don't have enough time can sometimes make you even less productive, because you're spending time obsessing over your lack of time instead of doing something with the time in front of you. Putting things in a schedule, ideally with sparkly gel pens, can help.

TWELVE

The night of *A Christmas Carol* is always my favorite of the school year and is only slightly marred this year by the fact that I keep needing to run to the bathroom to cry. I wouldn't say I'm a terribly nostalgic person, it's just when Abby asked for help getting her holly scrunchie on, I remembered making the first batch of Christmas ghost scrunchies freshman year, and how the first time I truly felt like I was part of the crew is when a bunch of us moving the Cratchits' table the next day winced in unison when it dug into the fresh hot glue burns on our fingers. Or when Essie asked for more safety pins for her Christmas Yet to Come's robes, and I started wondering who would be giving her safety pins for her costumes this time next year, and would they get the variety of sizes like I always did, or would she be stuck with gigantic pins popping open and stabbing her whenever she made a dramatic gesture? And so I would run to the single-stall bathroom and cry for just a little bit. I don't believe in crying in public. For myself, that is. I think everyone should have the space to express whatever emotions they're experiencing in front of everyone, and people bottling up emotion can lead to violent outbursts and bad screenplays. But crying in front of theater kids means having to explain your feelings, and that's just not something there's time for on opening night. Or something I'm interested in doing in general, opening night or not. I think I'm pretty self-aware, but that means I'm also self-aware enough to know I'm highly suggestible, and I don't want anyone else weighing in on potential reasons or remedies for my feelings when I know I've already figured them out.

I take stock of myself in the mirror. Everyone's eyes are a little blood-shot by opening night because of the whole crash-week lack of sleep, and I don't wear any mascara that would run anyway, so all I have to do to remove all evidence of my escalating sense of nostalgia leaking out of my eyes is thoroughly dry my cheeks. Satisfied, I swing the door open and walk almost directly into Sadie.

"I'm ready for my Christmas education. Blessed be the mistletoe. That's what you guys say, right? Hey, what's wrong?" she asks, suddenly looking at me more intently.

"Nothing's wrong. You should grab a seat—some of the parents like to come early and put down coats in whole sections to make sure they're covered if an aunt from the West Coast does show up. And every year, the coats seem to get bigger."

"Why were you crying?" Sadie asks, not taking the hint that I want to change the subject or looking away from my face. I almost say, "I wasn't." If Talley or Essie had asked, I would have said I wasn't, and I wouldn't have even thought of it as a lie. I always kind of thought of lies about your personal feelings as not actual lies. I think maybe because they never really seem to impact another person. Like, if I'm sad, and I tell you that I'm not sad, who's that going to hurt but me?

But staring at Sadie, I wonder. Doesn't it hurt someone to have a hurt friend, or a hurt girlfriend, and not have the information you need to try to help them? Maybe it hasn't come up before, because I can't remember Talley or Essie or anyone asking if I'd been crying. Which either means I'm really good at hiding, or they're really good at not noticing.

"I think the finality of senior year is hitting me," I say, with a smile, not because I'm trying to make myself look happier than I am, but because I am laughing at myself, just a little. I'm such a cliché, suddenly surprised that the end of high school means a million other little ends.

"Brian Lacosky, our first chair clarinet, started legitimately sobbing before our winter concert last week, and all we could get out of him was a shaky 'the last time I'll clean out a spit valve for the winter concert,'" Sadie says, pulling me into a hug. I know she's trying to be comforting by showing me I'm not the only one in danger of losing it whenever that graduation song my mom loves starts to play, but a part of me mostly wants her to say she'll miss parts of high school too. Her high school girlfriend, perhaps. Of course, we've only been dating for two and a half months, which means I only fill in about an eleventh of her high school pie chart, which seems like a very small section to get emotional about. And you also wouldn't get emotional about something ending in high school that wasn't actually ending in high school, right? But outside the single-stall bathroom five minutes away from "fifteen minutes to places" doesn't seem like the right time or place to have the "where do you see this going after graduation?" discussion.

"Well, I'm confident Brian Lacosky and I will get through this," I say instead. "Seriously, go get a seat. And if you think the drawstring of a puffer coat is sort of on a seat, someone's grandmother definitely thinks it's being saved for her."

Sadie smiles and pulls me into a kiss. Over the past few weeks, this has become the norm, a kiss before heading into opposite directions. I love that it feels like a choice every time, that even if I say something weird or awkward, or just not very interesting, she still wants to put her lips on mine, like she's re-upping our dating contract. And yes, there have been times, not at school but at my place and hers, when it isn't just one kiss, and she pushes into me, and there's a tiny catch in her breath when she pulls away that leaves me absolutely terrified that the next thing she's going to say is "Yeah, just kissing isn't going to be enough for me anymore."

But that isn't today, and I watch her walk off, wondering how the thought of one-eleventh of my high school pie chart possibly approaching an end makes me want to cry more than thinking about the end of every other piece of the chart put together.

———————

Three days after closing night, and I still wake up every morning to find pieces of glittering candy-cane-shaped confetti stuck to my checks. It's Christmas Eve, which means the last time before New Year's Eve that Brian and I are allowed to meet up with friends (or even text anybody) before Dad confiscates all our devices and locks them in the holiday family fun box. He's been doing this since early middle school when he saw some really cheesy made-for-TV movie where the teenagers were so consumed with texting they forgot the true meaning of Christmas and then murdered Santa Claus, I assume. (I never actually saw it, but Dad was pretty shaken up.)

I'm about to grab my phone when Brian comes flying through my bedroom door, dropping to the ground, then rolling to a stop at the edge of my bed.

"I might have ruined Christmas," he says, looking up at me before hanging his head with such force I'm momentarily open to the possibility he might have the ability to self-decapitate with the force of his shame alone (and, I think, a heavier-than-average head).

"Seems unlikely. Do you think you ruined it for all of humanity or just for . . . are you back with Allison?"

"Yes. And I got her bird earrings, because she likes birds. And I listen," he says.

"K. Who'd you ruin Christmas for, then?"

"Our family. I mean, probably mostly Dad, but he is—"

"I swear to god, if you say the head of this family—"

"No. The person in our family with the saddest eyes."

"True." I get out from under the covers and swing my legs over the side of the bed, trying to impress upon Brian he has my full attention.

"What'd you do?"

"It's not what I did do. It's what I forgot to do."

"Brian, I know you're still in final paper mode, but you do not have to speak in riddles to hit a word count in real-life conversations."

"Fine. I might have volunteered to do Mom's entire Christmas shopping list because I'm a very good son."

"Was this before or after you broke the washing machine by putting your cleats in it?"

"I've been a very good son for seventeen years. But the volunteering was after."

"And you didn't get Dad's stocking stuff?"

He shakes his head slowly.

"Well, I don't think CVS is going to be pleasant today, but if we leave now—"

"Or any not-stocking stuff."

"What?"

"I forgot to get his not-stocking stuff too."

"You didn't get Dad anything for Christmas."

"Right."

"Which in this case means you *and* Mom didn't get anything for Dad for Christmas."

"Yes."

"Which means our living room floor is going to be buried under presents for you, me, Mom, and contain exactly one signed *Back to the Future* poster I got Dad as proof that his family cares about him at all."

"Well, maybe you could give one of your speeches about the sad guy from the old play—"

"*Death of a Salesman* is about American capitalism leaving the individual behind. It says nothing about what happens to the individual when his family doesn't love him. How could you possibly forget to get Dad's presents? Our town is very good at reminding you every single second that Christmas is coming. The entire internet is also good at reminding you."

"That's why I remembered to get the bird earrings."

"Ooookay. Okay." I take a deep breath. This is fixable. We just need a plan. "So, you did not ruin Christmas, but you definitely ruined Christmas Eve. I'm supposed to meet up with Talley and Essie to watch Hallmark movies in four hours, and Sadie after that, which means I have about three hours to help you not crush our poor father's heart. Do you at least have the list Mom gave you?"

"Yes. Definitely somewhere in my room. Or somewhere in Mom and Dad's room. I'm not sure where the list is."

"Then we can wing it! We know Dad. And we know the limitations of the Westside strip mall. Be ready in fifteen minutes. You're driving. My playlists there and back," I say, swinging my legs back onto the bed and staring up at the ceiling as I listen to him retreat. I had all my Christmas shopping done by mid-November. I love Christmas music and lights and general glee, but I hate panic and pushing and the kind of anxiety that's so strong it can leak out of one person and drip onto another. So last-minute Christmas shopping is usually something I avoid at all costs. But Dad needs Christmas presents. I text Talley and Essie to tell them I might be a little late, and they promptly text back reminding me of my snack-bringing duties before going silent. I text Sadie next, explaining that our late-night gift exchange might turn into a midnight gift exchange, but that seems even more festive.

> Waited until the last minute to get my present?

> I would never procrastinate on something so important. My brother was charged with getting my dad's Christmas presents from my mom and forgot, so now we have to do some extreme holiday shopping and hope all those articles about the death of in-person retail were exaggerating.

That sounds horrible. Want some help?

I can't ask you to subject yourselves to so many minivans with Rudolph noses and their angry procrastinator drivers.

I'm volunteering. It'll be fun. Plus, after your brother outed both of you for skipping first-aid training back in middle school, I know that neither of you know how to properly splint an arm if things get too real in the electronics section. It would be irresponsible of me to let you go alone.

Fine. But you were warned. Meet us at my place in fifteen.

I smile at the screen. I hope she was just joking to even suggest I would have waited this long to get her gift. Back in November, she'd mentioned that she always hated the headshot she used for concerts in the social media promos and programs because the photo of her seated at the piano looks too stiff and lifeless.

"People already think classical music is boring. If I can actually get them to show up to a concert, I have a shot at showing them it's actually amazing and evocative and can be just as catchy as any song going viral on ReelLife. But no one can see that in this picture," she explained.

So I commissioned a watercolor artist I've followed for years to create a new illustrated headshot. I am not a visual artist, or an artist of any kind, so all I could do was hope that the painter I commissioned would find the description of what Sadie was looking for to be both helpful and not too prescriptive; I didn't want her to think I was treating her like an AI art generator or anything. But it turned out completely beautiful, and I have had to stop myself multiple times over the last month from giving it to her early, just so I could see her face when she opens it. I also got her a two-pound bag of gummy bears, her favorite, in the extremely unlikely case the picture doesn't land. It's important when gift giving to have a backup. It's important in life to have a backup, but gift giving in particular. That way, even on the off chance the second gift sucks too, they at least know it's because of your more generalized incompetence, and not your lack of caring about them, specifically. I couldn't stand it if Sadie thought, even for a second, that I don't care about her.

After a harrowing search for a parking space, during which Brian suggested, multiple times, that I could just jump out while the car was still moving to avoid getting honked at by the massive line of people doing drop-offs in front of Target, we're finally in the store, along with the rest of Connecticut. I wanted to stay together, because I believe that this situation calls for horror movie rules, but Sadie, ever brilliant, pointed out splitting up the list would mean we had a higher likelihood of getting out of here before New Year's. So I was in charge of getting Dad a suitcase record player. (He already has a massive one attached to an equally massive sound system, but apparently he and Mom had seen someone bring the suitcase version to the beach, and he seemed delighted by the portable possibilities.) I don't really get Dad's, or even some of my peers', obsession with records, which just makes your music bulkier and more breakable, but I am always impressed by album covers when I walk by a display or look through Dad's collection; the thumbnails on my phone never do the art justice. I'm transfixed by one for a band I've never heard of that has two elephants carrying an entire city perched between their trunks when I hear someone say, "Hey, Mia."

I turn around, and there's Ricky. Ricky is an incredibly sweet guy who everyone in drama would definitely love with no qualifiers if it wasn't for the fact that he is also incredibly talented at single-handedly destroying pieces of musical theater.

Drama has a strict "everyone who auditions at least gets to be in the ensemble" rule, which I, unlike Essie, completely support. Maybe it means there are some less-coordinated dancers or slightly off-key singers, but high school theater is about community, not winning Tonys.

Ricky, however, is a special case. Freshman year he put his foot in a piece of scenery during a pretty emotional number, which wouldn't have been that big a deal if he hadn't continued to dance, with the plywood and muslin bush stuck on his ankle like a very ill-designed garter, which caused him to give at least three of his fellow ensemble members some very nasty leg bruises by the time the number was done. It's still not clear to me whether he was honestly so in the zone that he didn't notice the bush, or if he misinterpreted the nuances of Mr. L's annual "the show must go on" speech, not realizing the show would very much go on, and would actually thrive, if one chorus member turned bush-humanoid discreetly left the stage. Every year we hoped and prayed Ricky would try out for a spring sport, since he was actually a jock two-thirds of the school year, and every February without fail he'd show up to auditions for the spring musical.

"Hey, Ricky. What's up?"

"Fixing a slight screwup with Talia's present. You met Talia at the cast party last year, right?"

"Yeah, she goes to St. Ann's?"

"Yup. And I bought her the perfect gift—this little heart-shaped waffle iron because she likes to make breakfast for dinner, and I figure all girls like hearts."

"Very gendered assumption. You found out she actually finds them corny?"

"No, they sent me a panini press instead."

"Paninis are fun."

"Yeah, but it's not specific, you know? Like, if we were doing a Secret Santa for basketball, a panini press would be fine, because it's a crowd-pleaser. But it doesn't say anything about Talia."

So, so sweet. So, so destructive.

"That's a good point. Did you find one here?"

"They're all out. I figured I'd go with a bunch of waffle toppings, and maybe some new headphones."

"Headphones because . . ."

"She always sets off the smoke alarm when she's cooking, and this way I figure she can drown it out. She'd notice if it was actually evacuation level with her other senses, right?"

"That's probably true. Maybe earbuds so she can leave one out, just in case? Anyway, I need to get back to my gift search—" I start.

"Hey, has Mr. L announced the spring musical yet?"

"Oh, uh, yeah, he actually told us during rehearsal last week. It's *Sweeney Todd*."

I hold my breath and hope he's going to talk about how excited he is to see it, safely tucked away in the audience.

"I love that movie!" He must see my horrified face at the idea that he thinks our musical will have anything to do with the Tim Burton adaptation because he quickly adds, "And I saw a production my cousin was in a few years back. I know there's a lot of competition, but I think I'm going to try out for Sweeney this year. I want to sing to some razors."

There is no danger of Ricky being cast as Sweeney. He has a decent voice, but we have a few senior guys who are ready to fight to the death for the lead. But I do have a sudden vision of Ricky the ensemble member somehow knocking into the tray of prop straight razors and said razors lodging in people's arms and legs. I mean, yes, technically they'll be completely dull and unable to give anyone so much as a paper cut. But everyone in drama has heard the urban legend of a school production getting "pranked" and having a rival school switch out the razors, which led to someone's actual onstage throat slitting.

"Oh, really? I just kind of figured you'd want to go for three sports senior year for college apps and everything," I gently attempt.

I have no idea whether colleges looking to collect jocks are also looking for multipronged jocks, but I figure maybe Ricky doesn't either.

"And miss the musical? No way." Ricky beams at me, undeterred. "I mean, Ms. Mitchell, the baseball coach, has been trying to recruit me, 'cause she knows I play the travel league in the summer—"

"The travel league that went to nationals last year? You were on it?" I ask. Even I remember the local news coverage and general team spirit at our town's two pizza places last summer.

"Yup. Camdon Cardinals all the way!"

"But you don't want to go out for the John Adams team?"

"Well, what would you guys do without me in *Sweeney*? I know you always need more baritones," he says, grinning. Honestly, he's basically a human sloth, just a nice smile and the inability to get out of anyone's way. And like the people who pick sloths off of busy roads so they don't hurt themselves or others, I realize I could be the one to actually *get* him out of everyone's way. Which wouldn't be selfish, because it would be helping so many other people. I'm pretty sure not even PETA criticized the sloth movers.

"Hey, Ricky, are you on ReelLife?"

"Sure. Have you seen that skateboarding basset hound? I thought for sure its ears were going to trip him up, but no. He's got it down."

"Huh, I'll have to check it out. But have you seen the account HeretoHelp?"

"No. But I don't really like those advice accounts much. I feel like they're always one step away from getting me to join a cult."

"No, I get it. I've just heard it's really helped some people in drama, onstage, at least, who are stressing over their audition song or whatever. Just thought it could be helpful."

"Oh. Cool. I'll look it up, then. Good luck with your gift search. And see you at auditions."

"Yup. I hope Talia loves the waffle stuff," I say, waving as he walks away. I start drafting the perfect targeted advice video in my head as soon as he's out of sight. Maybe something about playing to your strengths? Or possibly focusing on the many ways you can be a part of a theater community without actually doing any jazz hands. Anything to make sure Ricky would be putting on a uniform this spring instead of a costume.

———

Five hours later, Dad's presents have been acquired, wrapped, and put under the tree; Talley, Essie, and I have gotten through two and half Hallmark movies; and Sadie will be here any minute. I've wrapped her painting in sparkly blue paper with music notes dotted across it that I hope she'll think is thoughtful and not obvious. Brian is over at Allison's house giving her the bird earrings, and Mom and Dad have promised to give Sadie and me the downstairs for the night with minimal disruptions. I turn the Christmas tree lights on and watch the whole living room come alive with tiny pinpoints of multicolored light. I smooth out my skirt, part of a velvet red minidress that makes me feel like a successful business-woman from an '80s rom-com on her one night off. I know that might not be the go-to look for actually fashionable teenagers, but it makes me feel very competent, like I could go into a bar and order a martini and tell the bartender about my merger or something.

I look down to a text from Sadie saying she's here.

"You can come in," I call. I know it might seem rude not to meet her at the door, but I want her first sight of me tonight to be in the light of the

Christmas tree. I'm best at dramatic entrances when it's actually the other person entering, and I get to be perfectly still.

"Jesus, Mia. You look stunning," Sadie says as she walks in. I blush.

"Thank you. It's the multicolored lights, I'm pretty sure. Like how yellow makeup covers under-eye circles and green makeup covers zits, all the colored lights have hidden everything normally scary on my face."

"Hey, you know you don't have to do that every time I point out how beautiful you are. You can just bask in the compliment."

"Okay," I say. I don't think I could possibly accept "stunning" without a little self-deprecation, but it's nice that Sadie's giving me permission to try.

"So what Christmas activities have you planned for us? Are we going to have tiny fencing battles with candy canes? Wreath ring toss? Try to make a mathematical equation that could allow for Santa to hit at least all the houses in the state and send it to neighborhood kids?"

"I know your family doesn't do Christmas, but you've seen Christmas commercials at least."

"I have. And unless you've gotten me a giant gift-wrapped truck that's going to burst out of a forest, surely killing poor hibernating bunnies left and right, they've given me no insight into the holiday."

"Well, traditionally there's an exchanging of gifts."

"Sounds promising."

"Do you want yours now?"

"That depends. Is it traditional, in your Christmas culture, for the guest to receive her gift first?"

"No idea. But when my little second cousins come over on Christmas

Day, we give them their stuff first so they don't run around screaming 'presents.'"

"I can do that first if you want."

"I hope you like it," I say, handing her the very awkwardly wrapped gummy bear bag first. "This one is less exciting, just so you know."

I watch as she tears into the wrapping paper, and her eyes genuinely light up when she sees the gummy bear logo.

"I don't know what could possibly be more exciting than two pounds of sugar and red dye number two, but I trust you," she says, kissing my cheek. I haven't told her this, because it seems lame, but that is my favorite kind of kiss from her. It makes me feel like she's handling me very gently, carefully, and like at any second she might whisper a secret, something just between us, in my ear.

I hand her the picture and watch as she again turns the wrapping paper into confetti. For a moment, she just looks at it, no smile, but no look of horror either. I start to wonder if maybe she's confused, that it's so weird and maybe old-fashioned to give someone a commissioned portrait, it might need explanation.

"It's to use as a new headshot," I say quickly. "I mean, not that one, that's just to have, but the artist gave me a digital file, too, so whenever you need to give one for a new program or promo or whatever, you can send this one. If you like it."

"I love it," she says, finally, mercifully, smiling, not looking up at me but still staring at the picture. "All the color she put in the reflection off the piano is amazing. It's still a black piano, but there's more dimension. What picture were they working from?"

"Oh. I sent them a link to your website. But mostly I just explained what you didn't like about the headshots you already have. But you really like it?"

"I do. I can't believe you were paying such close attention to me bitching about a problem that isn't even a problem. Woe is me, I don't like how I look in a picture. But really, this is amazing."

She's quiet for a moment, just staring at the picture. I'm afraid she's found something wrong with it, and I'm about to explain I can totally return it (even if I'm pretty sure custom portraits are about as returnable as used toothbrushes) when she looks up at me and smiles, a truly glowing happiness radiating from her.

"It looks like me. I know it's stupid and small and probably vain, but I never think photos actually look like me. But this does. Mia, really, I love it."

She squeezes my hand, and I squeeze back, so happy and so relieved.

"So, now Christmas movies or . . . would you like your present, too?" she says, grinning.

"I am a little curious."

I watch as she pulls out a tiny box, about the size of two matchboxes stacked on top of each other, from her purse. It's wrapped in newspaper.

"For the environment," she explains pointing at the newspaper. "But I loved the music wrapping paper. I'm pretty sure if one person per couple does newspaper gift wrap, that's all the planet really needs." I smile, but make a mental note to only use recycled wrapping paper in the future.

I carefully unwrap and open the tiny box. Inside is one of those little hand-crank music boxes I remember seeing parents pull out at friends' birthday parties, leaving us all transfixed as we watched the scattered metal bumps along the cylinder produce a tinny-sounding "Happy Birthday."

"These things are adorable. Is it going to play a Christmas carol?"

"Try it out and see."

I pinch the tiny crank between my fingers and begin to turn it. The melody is pretty, light and sweet, but I don't recognize it. I turn the crank again, still smiling, but now panicking. If it's not a Christmas song, it must have some other significance I don't remember. Is it the first song Sadie ever played for me? A classical piece I had lied and said was my favorite in an effort to seem more worldly that now I couldn't even recognize? A famous love song that anyone with any kind of musical education would recognize as a romantic gesture?

"It's beautiful," I say, hoping this might prompt her to give some kind of hint about the song's title.

"You think?"

"Absolutely."

We sit in silence for a moment as I desperately scramble for some music-related adjectives I can use to fill the space between us.

"The tempo is nice, especially."

"Mia?"

"Yeah?"

"You're making it play fast or slow depending on how fast you crank it. You're in charge of the tempo."

"Yes. No, I meant it's so versatile. It would sound good at any tempo."

"I keep telling you I don't care that you haven't been studying music theory for the last twelve years. I don't know who won the little golden theater man last year—"

"Tonys are actually kind of hanging disks—"

"See? Not important. I know you're brilliant and wise, and if you want to learn some Chopin facts, I'm happy to give you some Chopin facts, but I also believe you can live a very happy life without them."

"I'm sorry. I don't know what the song is."

"Huh. That's weird. I think it says the title at the bottom of the box though."

I fish the slip of paper I hadn't even noticed out from the bottom of the box. Written in script and ringed with music notes—"Mia."

"There's a song called 'Mia'?"

"Well, now there is," Sadie says, looking at me expectantly. Now I definitely know there's something I'm missing.

"I wrote it," she clarifies. "For you. It's your song."

"You wrote me a song?"

"I did. And to be completely honest, writing songs for people—not hard for me. I could do the fake humble thing, but you know"—she points to herself—"child prodigy. Coming up with something that would sound decent on this thing, which I thought you'd like because it's small and cute, that was the challenge. But you're worth a challenge."

"You wrote me a song," I whisper. There are some other extremely sweet details in what she's just explained as well, but for the moment I'm hung up on this gesture. Someone created art for me, inspired by me. I'm a muse. I didn't think I would ever get to be a muse.

"I did. For your birthday I'll write you something a little longer and actually impressive. But I thought for Christmas you might want something that could be wrapped. Was I right?"

In response I turn the crank again and again. I feel the weight of Sadie as she leans into me and rips open the bag of gummy bears. She offers one to me, but I shake my head. I have to keep my hands free to turn the crank. I want to keep playing my song.

THIRTEEN

"Okay. Everyone trying out for a lead, please line up on the left side of the choir room. Everyone who wants to be considered for featured ensemble member role, on the right. And just a general reminder, candy conversation hearts are at least fifty percent chalk, and I have no scientific evidence to back this up, but I have seen more than one person cough up dust during an audition, so choose your stress snacks carefully," I say, spinning on the spot somewhat dramatically and sitting down behind the audition table next to Mr. L as I watch two freshmen techies take down everyone's name and voice part. Every year Mr. L insists on holding the auditions for the spring musical on Valentine's Day. I just figured it was a way to keep everything on a schedule, but I was there when Janie, the stage manager my sophomore year, asked him why he picked it and he explained, "I figured it would give the kids who didn't have anyone giving them candy a nice distraction, and any of them who were getting candy a lot of emotion to bring to the audition room."

I have no idea how he hasn't noticed in however many years this plan just takes an already stressful day and layers on heartbreak and blood-sugar spikes, but I thought it would be disrespectful to point that out. This was already my favorite Valentine's Day/audition day, because as stage manager I get to sit at the decision table with Mr. L and our music director, Ms. Verde, and because Sadie and I had exchanged flowers this morning so now I have a yellow pansy (thinking of you) tucked into my bun.

"Power corrupts, you know, Mia," Talley says, appearing suddenly by the side of the table.

"I'm allowed to watch the auditions and get Mr. L new pencils, not to offer any opinions of my own whatsoever," I point out. "I think I'm safe from corruption."

"I don't know. Do you get to pick the type of pencil? It always starts small. You'd know that if you watched more Marvel movies with me."

"You've made me watch all the Marvel movies."

"Well, obviously you're not watching them the right way. Hey, where's Essie? I wanted to wish her good luck. I even wrote it on a conversation heart."

"Uh," I say. Essie, of course, is not auditioning for the spring musical because it would conflict with her role in *Spring Awakening*, which she still doesn't think she's told me about and apparently still hadn't informed her boyfriend about either. She'd told me she had a chem test she had to make up and that Mr. L was letting her audition later, which was an almost comically ridiculous lie because (A) Mr. L never lets people audition at a different time—even if you were absent on audition day, he asked you to send in a video, and (B) that would be a very easy thing for me to casually fact-check with the person I was going to be sitting next to for the next two hours.

I had no idea if it was such a lazy lie because she wanted me to call her out on it or because she knew I was so trusting I'd just take her word for it (which, honestly, if I didn't have the information from her video, I probably would have). I also don't know what it means that she didn't make up any kind of lie for Talley, who she knows always shows up to wish her good luck before an audition. My mom always used to say if Brian and I left a really obvious clue to our childhood misdeeds (like a literal trail of cookie crumbs to one of our rooms), it was because we wanted to get caught, which never made sense to me. Who wants to get caught?

"She said she has to make up a chem test, and that she's going to audition for Mr. L later," I say. This is not a lie on my part, because it is what she said.

"Weird. Hey, did you get a chance to listen to my album last night?"

"I did," I say. "It was amazing." And it was. It was also twenty-two tracks he wanted me to listen to and be ready to critique basically overnight. But I knew it must be stressful to be waiting on someone's thoughts on something you poured your heart into, not sure if it would ever mean anything to anyone but you. "I'll get you the full report tonight, yeah?"

I do not mention the fact that tonight I'll also be creating the entire rehearsal schedule and working on my English essay on *Walden*, which was already kind of making me feel guilty for not appreciating trees enough in my daily life. I do not mention all of this because I don't want to make him feel like I see helping him as a chore or a burden. And possibly because I don't want to be seen as a complainer or whiner or anyone causing even the smallest amount of disruption. Which doesn't actually make me a doormat person, but someone who is very aware of what will make someone happy and what will make them melt into a puddle of anxiety.

"Did you see what Sadie got me?" I ask, pointing to the pansy. "And this," I add, holding out a copy of *The Language of Flowers*. I love it, not just because I thought there was something inherently romantic about speaking in code, but because it seems to imply a future of flowers I would need to understand.

"That's still happening, then?" he asks, not looking at me but staring intently at the two pencils he's currently air drumming with. I have no idea what he's referring to.

"What's still happening?"

"You and Sadie."

I barely know how to respond to such a bizarre question.

"You'd know if we had broken up, Talley. What kind of question is that?"

"No, it's great. I just, I don't know, never saw you as a relationship type of person, you know?"

The list of kinds of people Talley doesn't see me as is growing.

"Not all relationships are about sex," I say, hopefully not too defensively.

"No, it's not about you being ace. You know Greg, from that jazz band I was in last summer, is ace, and he's had, like, a girlfriend a semester. I just mean . . ."

"You just mean what? That I'm so off-putting as a person you never thought anyone would willingly date me?" I try to laugh at the end, to make this a joke, but it suddenly feels like a very serious question.

"I guess I just always kind of saw you as kind of solitary, you know?"

"How solitary can I be if I'm always hanging out with you and Essie?"

"But that doesn't count."

"Because you're both figments of my imagination? Is this the moment I find out no one else can see Brad Pitt?" I normally wouldn't use a *Fight Club* reference in my day-to-day life, but Brian had been watching it last night, and my brain was scrambling to convince me my best friend wasn't trying to tell me he pictured me as some kind of sad-eyed hermit. A sad-eyed hermit without any kind of life purpose or any romantic prospects. Who was always on call to read his song lyrics, talk through a question on his science homework, fill the space he didn't seem to know how to fill on his own.

"You're going to take this the wrong way."

"Is what people say before they say something really mean."

"Never mind," he says, walking toward the door.

"Talley, you can't just let me sit here thinking about what you're too afraid to explain about how you see me. Come on."

"I guess it's hard for me to picture you hanging out, just talking and chilling with someone who isn't us, you know? One-on-one. But you are, and it's cool. Let me know what you think of the track order, by the way. I was so stuck, I ended doing them alphabetically, and that can't be the best option, right?" he calls as he heads out the door.

Sometimes, at moments when I'm feeling not great about myself—about how I have watched enough curly-girl-method videos to match the run time of *Titanic* and still can't manage to de-puff my hair, or how I've never really felt like one of my observations in a class has made a teacher feel like they made the right choice trying to educate the next generation—I spiral into wondering how much of my friendship with Talley and Essie is accidental. Not on my part. But if someone else had been put in their lab group in sixth grade, would they be just as happy having that person be their sounding board?

"Mia." Micha, one of the freshmen, interrupts my thoughts and I jump. "We've got the list of people trying out for leads and the ones for featured ensemble. Who do you guys want to hear first?"

"Ask Mr. L," I say. "I'm going to go get some water. Just take whatever group he wants second out in the hall, and remind everyone this is not a soundproof room, so if they want to warm up or rehearse something, they'll have to go outside, okay?"

He nods, and I walk out into the hall that connects the choir room to backstage. If I have to fit writing Talley's critique into my schedule for tonight as well, I should really start working on my essay. I can always sit at the table for the second half. Plus, what if Talley's right, and just sitting behind that desk flips some kind of switch in my brain and suddenly turns me into the kind of stage manager who has the lower techies bring me a daily Frappuccino? I'm about to sit on the stairs and pull out my book when I hear the faint but unmistakable sound of someone crying backstage, far enough from the choir room that no one in auditions would hear it.

I approach the sound slowly, walking gingerly so a floorboard squeak doesn't scare whoever's back there.

"Hey, you okay? I can go if you just want to be alone, no problem. I just want to make sure you're all right."

"I'm sorry," the voice says. "I didn't mean to be so loud. Am I disturbing auditions?"

"No, I only heard you from the hallway. You're not disturbing anyone. But I volunteer to be disturbed, if you want to talk?"

The curtain pulls back, and I see Maria, a junior who was already seen as serious competition for the starring role of Mrs. Lovett even before anyone noticed Essie wasn't trying out. Her face is covered in an incredibly messy mixture of makeup that tells me not only has she been crying for a long time, but she's made no attempt to clean her face up between crying jags. Which means she's probably been hiding for a while, too.

"Did I miss auditions?" she asks, without any indication in her tone that she'd actually be upset if she did.

"No, they're just getting started. What's up?"

"Don't you have a guess?" she asks. I did, but I didn't want to say it. Maria was the most talented singer we had, after Essie, but she had a bigger rep for running out of rehearsal in tears because her asshole boyfriend texted her something that showcased exactly how big an asshole he is.

"James forgot Valentine's Day?" I suggest. This wasn't a real guess, as a lack of Valentine's Day gift would be a spectacular upgrade from last year when he presented her, in front of all of drama, with a gift basket full of that fake weight-loss tea.

"He did not. He didn't get me tea this year, at least."

"That's good," I say, because it seems like what you should say to comfort someone whose boyfriend is a complete asshole. "Please, *please*, dump him to save yourself and, to a lesser degree, us" would be rude and might make her cry harder, which I really wanted to avoid.

"He did get me a gift certificate for a spa day."

"Oh. That's kind of sweet, right?"

"The package he got was a full body wax, and when he gave it to me, he said he wanted me to use it before he comes on this spring break trip with my family so he won't be embarrassed to be seen with me."

"And you're crying because you immediately dumped him, and

even though that was the right decision, ending a relationship is always emotional?"

This does make her cry harder, something I probably could have predicted even if I hoped it would have sparked a moment of clarity for her. I pat her on the knee to let her know I'll wait until she's ready to talk again.

"How could I just end things?" she chokes out after a few minutes.

"With a text. Or skywriting, if you have some extra cash. Or I could do it for you. Want me to do it for you?" I'm so outraged on her behalf, energized by it, that that option doesn't even seem so horrible. I've never dumped someone before, and most likely never will, because that sounds like one of the most intense forms of interpersonal conflict you can have, and I like to avoid those, but doing it for someone else seems like a way to have an essential human experience without having a panic attack. Plus, I'd be saving Maria from ending up in one of those viral mean groom videos where the guy doesn't just smash the wedding cake on his bride's face, but does it with such force and anger, he should probably be charged with assault.

"We've been together since freshman year," she says.

"Which means you've put up with him being awful for almost three years."

"I know he can be cruel in these big public moments. But when it's just the two of us, he can be really sweet."

"So he just likes to humiliate you in public, not in private."

"Mia . . ."

"Maria, what will convince you to break up with him? Is it more people saying exactly what I'm saying? Because I already have everyone lined up outside for auditions. I could just bring them inside and have them explain, one by one, why he's awful and how your life would be so much better without him."

"No, that's okay," she says, laughing unconvincingly and fishing a makeup wipe out of her bag, dragging it across her face to get the clumps of mascara and eye shadow off her cheeks.

"I'm just being stupid," she says, getting up. "Thanks for listening, Mia. I've got to get in line for auditions."

"It's not stupid to cry when the person who's supposed to love you is being cruel. And it's not stupid to stay, but it is *tragically misguided*." I have to half yell since she's already halfway to the choir room door. I can't let her leave like this. I can't let her go into another Valentine's Day, or any day, with a guy who's convincing her she needs to change something about herself to be loved. She's in too deep to see clearly, but I can help her fix this, even if she can't see that. I chase after her.

"Hey, Maria, wait! Have you ever heard of that advice ReelLife account HeretoHelp?"

———

My phone buzzes off the too-tall stack of books on my desk and falls to the floor. I have to stop putting it on such precarious places. I pick it up to see it's Essie. I wonder, briefly, if she's going to try to tell me how her makeup chem test went.

"Hey. How'd auditions go?"

"Pretty good. Alex and Micky brought actual straight razors for their songs, and Mr. L had to look up in the school handbook whether they're classified as a weapon, which they're not, by the way. Otherwise uneventful. When are you doing your audition?"

"Actually, I'm not," she says. I prepare myself to act surprised by her *Spring Awakening* news, while making sure she knows I'm excited for her success. I know the situation isn't great for a bunch of reasons, but it is nice to be able to feel so prepared for something so spontaneous.

"I have to skip the spring musical to help my mom at the restaurant."

"What? I mean, why?" I ask. On its face, that sounds a little insensitive, as the obvious answer is her mom's pizza place is struggling enough that she has to demand her daughter work there for free, giving up her senior musical out of a sense of filial obligation. But I also know that's not true.

"I guess things have been tighter than she was letting me know, but she's just been so stressed out lately, and since I already got into Tisch on early admission, I figure this is my last chance to really help her out before I abandon her for the stage, you know?"

Talley would say you're already abandoning him for the stage, I think. But instead I just say, "Still, senior-year musical. Won't you go into some kind of acting withdrawal?" This would be a bitchy thing to say if she really was being selfless, but I know she's lying. And I want to give her every opportunity to come clean. To not lean into this lie. To just to talk to me. Maybe Mom was right, and the crumbs leading to the truth mean deep down she wants to be caught.

"I'll be fine. I'll have Mom play lots of show tunes while I work. Maybe I'll start standing on the counter and performing, like that diner we saw on ReelLife."

Or maybe she's like most liars, and she doesn't actually want to be caught at all. It's a good lie. It has a kind of emotional protective bubble, something people won't want to ask follow-up questions about, but she also has answers to follow-up questions, obviously pre-prepared. It's possible Essie is a very good liar.

"Did you tell Talley?"

"Yeah. And I told him I'm going to probably have to miss prom. Because, you know, a weekend night in the spring is when it gets really crazy. But we already went to junior prom, and we have enough pictures of us together, you know?"

It's not a bad argument. But it's an incomplete argument. I decide to try one last tactic to try to convince Essie to open up—confessing something of my own.

"Hey, so, I kind of wanted your advice about something. Sadie has been so great and supportive, and not pressuring at all about the whole no sex or really even sex-adjacent stuff. And it's not like I think that's going to change or anything. But I kind of think I want to get prepared to be ready to try things, maybe. I don't know, maybe I should start watching the sexy parts in movies I always fast-forward over? What ones do you think I should start with—"

"Hey, Mia, I've got to go. Mom wants me to grab a shift tonight so I'll text you later."

She hangs up, and I stare at the phone for a minute. I really thought that might work, presenting my own problem first. And it would have been really nice to think she cared about helping me with my problems as much as I cared about helping her with hers.

FOURTEEN

Sometimes I really wish we had a bigger drama club budget. Or any budget, really. I found out, sort of on accident during a prop run at the dollar store, that Mr. L has been personally paying for any costumes or props we don't already have in storage out of his own pocket for years. Which is why I didn't even consider asking if we could buy actual squibs, the things real theaters use when you need a realistic blood spray, and I'm instead experimenting with watered-down ketchup vs. corn syrup and food dye I'm putting in tiny ziplock bags, with an extra seal of hot glue, all stolen from the home ec supply closet for maximum thriftiness (and by stolen, I mean I promised to clean the kitchen stations for a week in exchange). I can hear rehearsal on the other side of the curtain, the ensemble asking the audience to attend the tale of Sweeney Todd (which, no offense to Mr. Sondheim, I always thought was kind of redundant since everyone in the audience had already obviously decided to attend the tale).

"Mia." A freshman techie pokes their head in.

"Which looks more like blood?" I ask before she can say anything else, piercing each bag with a safety pin and letting them both drip on two sides of a white piece of cloth.

"Um, neither make me want to throw up, and I almost always throw up when I see real blood, if that helps?" she says.

It does, not exactly in my experiment, but now I know to keep her up in the booth, away from what will eventually be my hyperrealistic blood for the actual performances.

"Yes. Thanks. Did you need me?"

"Yeah. Mr. L says he needs to talk to all of us."

I'm immediately alarmed. Partially because alarm is one of my go-to emotions, and partially because Mr. L never talks to us all. I actually think he might be the only drama teacher in America who's afraid of public speaking. He prefers to watch, then take small groups aside, and when he has sweeping notes, he normally lets one of the techies send out an email. I'm pretty sure the last time he talked to all of us was sophomore year when one of the seniors (and leads) was banned from all after-school activities because of his GPA, and he had to rally us all to collectively tutor him.

I find Essie sitting on the edge of the stage and sit next to her. She'll show up to a rehearsal every few weeks. Even though she's not a part of the musical, she's still a drama club senior, and no one, not even Mr. L, would think to kick her out. I can't tell, when she watches a run-through, if she regrets her decision, or if she already feels a million miles away from being in a high school show.

"Any idea what this is about?" she asks.

"No idea," I say, just as Mr. L starts clearing his throat. He's visibly sweating, and I hope whatever he has to say is quick, because I'm afraid he's going to pass out, and we'll get to see if that freshman was lying or not about their blood-vomit connection.

"All right, everybody. Now I want to start off saying: She is okay, she's going to be okay, but Jessica was in a car accident last night."

A murmuring starts almost immediately, a combination, I'm sure, of genuine concern and speculation. Jessica is well-liked, but people are always curious about the potential slipups of straight-A students.

"What happened, Mr. L?" George, a.k.a. Mr. Pirelli, asks. I figure it might be the villainous mustache he's insisted on wearing during the entire rehearsal process that makes me think he's more interested in something salacious than Jessica's actual well-being.

"Her mother has allowed me to share that Jessica fell asleep at the wheel. She said she wanted to remind you all that it's dangerous, especially at your age, to overextend yourselves, and that padding your college application isn't worth risking your life." He clears his throat and gives us all a pointed look, scanning the crowd like he's trying to find the most at-risk overachievers. "All right, if you'd like information on how to visit Jessica, you can see me; otherwise, you're dismissed for the day."

Essie is saying something about collecting money for an Edible Arrangement, but I can't really hear her. Because I remember the video I sent Jessica in November. The video I sent after she talked about being swamped, exhausted, spread too thin. The video that *didn't* involve telling her to cut back on her responsibilities but to bullet journal. I nod at Essie, saying something encouraging but noncommittal about her get-well gift idea, then walk out off the stage in a kind of trance. Because Jessica is in the hospital, and I'm pretty sure it's all my fault.

FIFTEEN

I knew I should go visit Jessica. To apologize. To beg forgiveness. But I was too afraid and had too many excuses at my disposal—teachers were starting to pile on end-of-the-year projects, and things with the musical were starting to get busy. I had to make sure a prop was fixed, a costume piece was sourced, a set piece was painted. I wonder how many busy people were just using a packed to-do list to avoid the one thing they really should do.

I was completely avoiding HeretoHelp too. Every video request seemed like another potential way I could hurt someone. But even knowing what it had done, what I had done, I couldn't bring myself to delete it entirely. Because as guilty as I felt, it was hard not to think about my successes too. Ricky actually did skip auditions after watching my video on sticking to your strengths. (In a show of more cosmic gratitude, I even organized a group drama outing to one of his baseball games. We definitely had the best-crafted cheers.) I helped one of the techies with their fear of snakes (less about conquering the fear and more about arming themselves with information—there aren't really many poisonous snakes hanging out in Connecticut), and I had convinced Kelly, who's playing Johanna (and using Johanna as her ReelLife screen name), to actually *tell* her girlfriend she wanted to take a break (instead of her original plan, which according to the video, she had dubbed very, very slow ghosting). Maybe all the people I helped would karmically make up for Jessica. I don't think I really believe that, but opening the app still feels almost instinctual to me. This time, I have one new video message. I open it and press play. I don't need to respond, but it couldn't hurt to see what the question was.

"I don't know how to tell my girlfriend, I mean I don't know how to tell anybody, I didn't get into college. Not my top-choice college. Or my top tier or whatever. No colleges at all."

I pause it for a second. That would be tough. I wonder if I've finally shown up on someone's page beyond the bounds of John Adams High, because our guidance counselor has been really good about impressing on us just how important applying to a few safety schools is, no matter how confident we were that we'd get into our top choices. I hit play again.

"I know you're probably thinking, didn't you apply to any safety schools?" The figure, who has a kind of dragon filter on, lets out a deep sigh, expelling smoke from the dragon's mouth.

"So my girlfriend and I had this plan to go to school together in New York City. She got into her top choice, and I promised I'd apply to only schools in New York City too. And I did. But I figured it would be kind of silly to pay out-of-state tuition for a state school, so I just applied to the kind-of-fancy city schools. But I don't really have fancy city school grades. Or SAT scores. Or extracurriculars, except pit band and creating albums with one and a half too many tracks."

I pause the video again, this time in shock. It's Talley. I had the suspicion at the New York City plan, but more than one person could want to go to school with their girlfriend in New York City. More than one person could have grades Essie was always giving him a hard time about and a refusal to take the SATs more than once. But that line about one and half too many tracks . . . was mine. From one of my most recent album reports.

Talley hadn't gotten into college. Which I knew would crush him, but . . . why was he here, on an app, asking for advice, instead of talking to his friends? Essie and I would help him deal. We'd make sure he was okay. Of course, comforting him through this would only work if he actually told us. I hit unpause on the video yet again.

"So now I've completely screwed up the plan. And any other future plans I had besides busking on the subway. I don't know how to tell her. Should I tell her? Maybe I can just get an apartment in the city and pretend to be living in the dorm? It could be kind of fun to come up with fake classes and fake roommate drama . . ." Talley the dragon trails off.

I've sworn off advice giving for a while, but this isn't one I can ignore. I don't need any extra time to plan my response video. I just have to hope he's ready to hear my advice. Or I guess I know he's not ready to hear *my* advice, but I can't think about that right now. Helping him is more important than the anger that might have been collecting ever since we spoke about the various things he doesn't believe I'm capable of. I stack up my books, put my phone on the makeshift stand with a little more force than needed, and hit record.

"The one thing that never fixes one lie is coming up with more lies."

Secrets, on the other hand . . . those could be more complicated.

SIXTEEN

It seems like forever since the three of us have hung out, what with Essie always "helping her mom" (a.k.a. being in rehearsal), and Talley, I assume, trying to buy fake student ID badges off the deep web, because even though I had responded to his video question a full three days ago, he hadn't confessed to (actual) me; and based on the fact that Essie was currently holding his hand and looking at him like all their future plans would soon be realized, I'm pretty sure he hasn't told her either. I managed to convince them to get frozen yogurt on a Thursday by pointing out we hadn't done anything to show we were seniors able to slack just a little all spring, and then I proceeded to spend the whole time trying to bring up musical theater about troubled youths and the punishing world of college admissions in an organic way, and failing miserably. Walking out of the fro-yo place with them, I've decided to give myself a momentary reprieve from trying to get my friends to actually talk to me (or each other) and just enjoy being together, in our town, on a weeknight. For all I know, it could be one of the smaller, subtler lasts for us.

Turning the corner, I think I see the poster before Talley or Essie, though the delay is only a second or two. Then they're both seeing it, stuck right in the middle of the community bulletin board on the corner, covering up all the ads for math tutors and dog walkers: "Come to Westside Theater's Production of *Spring Awakening*," with dates that include prom and a beaming, nineteenth-century-clad Essie just to the left of the two leads. Both Essie and Talley stop dead.

"What is this?" Talley asks. But I can tell from his tone he's not actually confused. Talley is literally very aware of what this is. He just can't believe what it is.

"Talley—" Essie starts.

"So this is what you've been doing, not helping your mom?"

"I knew you'd get mad—don't get mad."

"Talley, just hear her out," I interject.

Then Talley's not looking at the poster or Essie anymore. He's looking at me. He's staring at me like I'm a sudoku puzzle he's this close to figuring out.

"You aren't surprised." Talley whispers so quietly, I don't think I've heard him right.

"What?" I ask.

"You aren't surprised by the poster. Did Essie tell you?"

He turns to her.

"Did you tell everybody but me?"

"I haven't told anyone! Including Mia," Essie insists.

"Everyone knows but your idiot boyfriend!" Talley says, shouting now.

"Talley, come on, let her explain," I try.

"Explain why she's been lying to me for months? Explain how she didn't tell me she was making this giant life decision, and what that says about our promise to make those kinds of decisions together?"

He's getting louder, and people are staring at us, and I hate that I can feel so many eyes on us, and I'm kind of angry at Talley for making people stare at us, which is maybe why I spit out, without thinking, "Well, you made a pretty big decision without telling her too."

My hand goes over my mouth instantly, like I can stuff the words back in.

"What?" Essie asks. But I'm not looking at her. I'm looking at Talley. Who's staring at me. After what seems like forever, he slowly turns to Essie.

"Did you ask HeretoHelp for advice about taking the part?"

I can feel my heartbeat thrumming through every inch of my body.

"How did you—?" Essie starts to ask.

"What did they say? You asked for advice about taking the part—what did they say?"

"They told me I'd regret it if I didn't take the part. But that doesn't mean that some piece of me doesn't regret—"

"It's Mia," Talley says, in a voice so completely flat, it barely sounds like his. I'm not moving. I can't move. If I don't move, maybe everything else will stop moving too.

"What's Mia?" Essie says, looking from Talley to me in complete confusion.

"She's HeretoHelp. She told you to take the part. Did you know it was her?" he says, pivoting suddenly to me.

"Talley," I say. And then stop. I say his name like it's a magic word that will break the spell, and he'll stop looking at me like I'm a stranger, like

I'm someone he'd be happy never to see again.

"Talley, I know you're pissed, but accusing Mia," Essie starts, and my hearts swells and freezes in equal measure, so happy Essie is defending me, so terrified that she might never come to my defense ever again once she learns the truth.

He's staring at me again, an expression on his face like he's trying to solve a calculus problem.

"Do you remember everyone complaining about HeretoHelp's holiday blackout?" he says, slowly. "Christmas Day through New Year's Eve? Who logs off for a whole week just when they're starting to build a following? Who takes a break from tech right before New Year's resolutions start, when everyone seems to be doing nothing but lying on the couch scrolling? Who would, unless their phone was locked in a drawer in their parents' room?"

"Talley, people take holiday breaks, I don't think this is the smoking gun you think it is—"

"And you knew it was me," he says, turning back to me, "right?"

I nod, because I don't know what else to do.

"Maybe you wanted to get caught? Or you just think we're all really, really dumb. But I guess we have been this whole time. I mean, I didn't figure it out. A lot of famous people didn't go to college. A lot of famous musicians. HeretoHelp just happened to name-drop my three favorites?"

"I wanted you to feel hopeful," I whisper, even though I know he's figured it out, because even through his anger that I didn't tell him about Essie, he must know that I wasn't focusing on my anonymity when I was making that video because all my energy was going into making sure he knew he was going to be okay. I guess minus the energy convincing myself

I shouldn't take it too personally that he didn't feel comfortable coming to actual me for advice.

Essie is now looking at me too, eyes wide in disbelief.

"He's right? HeretoHelp is you?"

I nod again.

"Mia, what the absolute fuck is wrong with you?"

This is not the first time Essie has said this to me. But before, it's always been with an air of parental condescension. Like, oh, silly little Mia doesn't know exactly what she wants to do with the rest of her life, what are we going to do with her?

"I know, I should have told you guys, but staying anonymous was kind of the point, and not a lot of things stay anonymous in drama when you guys know about it."

"That's not what . . ." Essie pauses, looks down, then flicks her eyes up. The fact that it's so understated is what makes it so unnerving. Essie is never understated.

"Talley's right, isn't he? You knew it was me, too. You saw through everyone's filters, everyone in drama."

I nod. "Now we just have to decide if it was my powers of deduction or the power of friendship, right?" I say, attempting a smile.

"Oh my god, Mia, go actually fuck yourself," Talley says, in a way that makes me feel like he's slapped me. I think I might have literally flinched. No one has ever talked to me like that. I can barely take the tension when someone says something like that on a TV show. And whenever I took the time to mentally catalog all the things I should be worried about in the future, dealing with someone I love talking to me like that never came up, because I'd never give them a reason to.

"Talley, I said I was sorry. I know I should have told you about Essie—"

"Essie's lie is its own thing—this is about you sitting in your room and being a goddamn puppet master! We, not just Essie and me, everyone at drama thought we were coming to someone for advice who could be totally objective. Not someone who stood to gain something from pushing us in a certain direction."

All I can do for a moment is stare at him.

"How exactly does me telling Essie to chase her dream and flat-out comforting you help me gain anything?"

"You made a video for Maria, didn't you?" Essie says. "That's why she broke up with James. She said she found some advice that really spoke to her. One less thing to deal with during rehearsals, right?"

The sick feeling is pushed out just a little by a flicker of anger.

"Yes, I'm so sorry for telling Maria what literally everybody was too scared to—that James was toxic, and she would be so much better off without him, so she could be *happy*. Sometimes when someone's entire life gets better, they do cry less in public. Should I have told her to ask him to prom?"

"And Ricky," Talley says, not looking at me, but at his feet. "You told him he should go out for baseball this year so you wouldn't have to explain why he only made the ensemble again?"

"I told someone who's good at sports and has been murdering jazz squares, which I didn't think was humanly possible, to stick with his strengths. Another crime against humanity."

"You don't even see it, do you? How messed up it is that you could use things you knew about them against them, to manipulate them into doing exactly what you wanted them to do?"

"Right, because the only way I could possibly convince anyone to do anything is through mind games and witchcraft, right? No one would possibly take my advice at face value, because who would listen to what I have to say, right? Why would anyone listen to Mia?!"

I'm screaming now, and I don't care. They're listening to me, and they know who I am, and suddenly I don't care about their anger because mine is so big, it's crowding everything else out.

"You went to a stranger on an app instead of coming to me. Why? Don't you trust me? Don't you care about what I think?"

"Maybe I would have called if you hadn't been so busy with Sadie," Essie says, the whine in her voice suddenly nails on a chalkboard. How dare she bring Sadie into this, someone who has always, always been there for me. Whose only crime might be showing the kind of care and attention I had been missing in my other relationships.

"Absolutely fucking not. I never, ever ditched you for one second. I will not apologize for finding someone who loves me—"

And then Talley is laughing. In my head it's the cold clear laugh of a serial killer, but I know it's probably just his normal laugh heard through this weird haze of rage. Essie looks nervous suddenly, her eyes darting back between Talley and me.

"Talley, don't—" she starts.

"Not listening to you right now, Essie. Besides, Mia thinks we don't care what she thinks. We should ask for her advice, right? Mia, if you had a friend who was in the first romantic relationship she's ever had, and you found out her new girlfriend was using her as a human chastity belt, would you share that information, or would you sit on it for months because she's too fragile? Or did you say too breakable, babe? I don't want to misquote you."

"What are you talking about?" I ask. My head is buzzing like it does during a Spanish quiz, the meaning of words just beyond my reach as I will them to slot into sentences.

"Mia, we were honestly just trying to protect you—" Essie starts.

"But it's obvious you don't need that kind of protecting," Talley interrupts, his voice hard. "I was standing behind Sadie at my brother's concert in November. I was about to tap her on the shoulder and say hi when I heard what she was telling her friend. That she was dating this ace girl at her new school. And when her friend said that must be hard for Sex Fiend Sadie, she said that that's the point—how else was she going to win the abstinence bet with her brother?"

I can't feel my hands. I feel like my whole body is going numb. I try to grasp at words, at a joke that will make this go away, make it something laughable, dismissible.

"Abstinence bet? Seriously, Talley, you're so mad at me, you're going to cast my girlfriend in some weird teen movie from the early 2000s? Is she also going to take my virginity on the eve of Y2K or something?"

"Mitch and Micheal were with him. They heard it too. Text them, if you want," Essie says, and if she had said it jeeringly, maybe I could have rationalized it, assumed she was lashing out, making something up because she was angry. Maybe even so my relationship would implode just like hers seems to be. But she says it sadly. I can feel my hands cupping my face, and I don't know when I started. It just feels necessary if I want to be completely sure my head isn't going to fly clean off my body.

"Why would she say that?" I whisper.

"Because that's what she's doing. Using you. That's what people do in general, actually," Talley says, looking from me to Essie. I almost want to make fun of him for how dramatic it sounds, but every word he's saying hits a little too hard.

"You have to tell everyone. Today," Essie says. It takes me a second to realize she's not talking about Sadie, but HeretoHelp. Which seems almost comically inconsequential in the face of this new information about Sadie, which I'm still willing to be not true, not true, not true.

"You know, that was always the plan," I say, grabbing my coat and my bag as I speak. "Well, technically the plan was going to be to tell everyone opening night of *Sweeney*, but it's not like I wasn't ever going to tell you. In fact, I wanted to tell you. Wanted to tell everyone that I've been fixing your problems. And that they could have been fixed continuously for the last four years if anyone would actually just listen to me."

I don't think about it in the moment. But there is the shadow of a thought, something in my head, possibly Addy's voice, saying, "You talk a big advice game, but can you really be that righteous about it if you don't say the whole truth?"

"Neither of you were trying to protect the other," I say, not quietly, but not shouting either. With authority. Because I am the foremost authority on the dysfunction of Talley and Essie. "You were trying to protect yourself. Neither of you wants to be the one who has to say it—you're eighteen and you've been together for five years, and it's more than the logistics that are getting in the way. You don't know who you are if you're not half of Talley and Essie. And for the first time, you're both curious. And I wish you luck working through that reality, because neither of you have a friend capable of listening to someone else's problems for more than five minutes besides me, and you don't have me anymore."

I don't turn to look at their expressions. I don't pause to see if they come up with a retort. I simply walk away.

I'm not even sure I make the conscious decision to go, but twenty minutes after my possibly friendship-ending fight, I find myself standing in front of the door to Jessica's hospital room. Maybe I go because I figure things can't possibly get worse. Or maybe I go because I *want* them to. To punish myself. To see if I can reach a kind of critical mass of guilt and anger and sadness that then cancels everything out so I can just feel nothing, even just for a minute.

Or maybe it's because even though I don't feel like I owe Talley and Essie much of anything at the moment, I know I owe it to Jessica to unmask myself in person—and to apologize.

I stand in the hallway awkwardly for a moment and take a look at the exact toll my awful advice has taken. Her face is a horrible mix of purple and green, with a deep red cut slashed across her forehead. Eventually she looks up.

"Oh, hey, Mia. What's up?"

I can tell Jessica is a little surprised. It's not like we're super close. Or maybe I'm the only asshole who didn't text before showing up to visit her.

"I brought you a mocha latte," I say, waving the foamy drink a little, just enough so it dribbles onto my hand.

"You're a little late. I needed the caffeine Friday night."

"Oh, my god, I didn't even . . . I'm not mocking you, or . . . oh my god."

"Mia. It's a joke. I would love a mocha latte. A lot more than all the flower arrangements actually."

"Okay. Great. Here you go," I say, kind of sidestepping toward her bed until I'm close enough to pass it to her. I have no idea why I'm moving this way. It's possible my guilt is now so heavy, it's impacting my ability to walk.

"I'll be back in time for crash week, you know. If you're worried about being out a madwoman. I might actually need less makeup now, with my face already so screwed up. But the doctor did give me the okay."

I nod. She thinks I'm here to check something off about the play. Does she really think I'd care more about a production running smoothly than her?

"You probably know Essie and Talley did a singing get-well card? It was a hit. Nurses came to watch from different floors."

I nod again. I feel her eyes on me, judging me, rightfully, for making the recently concussed person drive the conversation.

"It's my fault," I blurt out. It's not what I plan to do, but I feel less sick almost immediately. Still a little sick, sure, but maybe right *after* the old-timey doctor says I'm out of danger instead of before.

"The singing get-well card?" Jessica asks, looking confused. God-damn it. I'd gotten so in my head, I didn't think about the *placement* of my blunt confession.

"Your accident," I clarify. Then I just let her process that. Go through options. Calling the police for, I'm just guessing, reckless endangerment through digital advice. (It had been a while since I've watched *Law and Order* with Dad, so I'm not completely up-to-date on social media crime statutes.) Making a scathing post about my complete lack of human feeling that would spread so widely I'd be asked to appear on the *Today* show on a segment on evil teenagers.

"I don't . . . think so? Unless you're the one who signed me up for six AP classes. But I'm pretty sure that was me."

"I'm HeretoHelp."

Jessica stares back at me, obviously with no idea what I'm talking about. Which makes sense—she does have head trauma.

"The advice account? You sent it, I mean, me, a message asking for advice on feeling overwhelmed. And I told you to bullet journal."

"Oh yeah. That was . . . November? Wait, that means you're the one who told Bobby to break up with his long-distance girlfriend, right? That's kind of impressive. You saved us from a lot of really bad Instagram poetry."

She's obviously not getting this. And any effort I make to clarify the fact that we should not be chatting about my good advice but instead she should be dragging me for my horrible advice seems like it would make things even worse. But I have to try.

"I didn't realize you were struggling, even though I should've, and the advice I gave was so, so not what you needed, and probably just convinced you that you had to organize things instead of take on less. I should have told you to take on less—"

"Mia, you think I continued on a self-destructive perfectionist near-death spiral that probably started when I got my first perfect score on a spelling test in first grade because sometime before winter break someone I didn't know on the internet didn't tell me I was going to burn out?"

"It could have maybe made you look at things differently—"

"No, Mia, it wouldn't have. Because my mom telling me to drop down to honors didn't, and Tyler literally dumping out my Red Bull when

165

I wasn't looking in the hopes that maybe I'd accidentally fall into some rest didn't. I—Listen, I don't want to sound mean. But what makes you think I'd listen to you?"

"I did see you with a bullet journal afterward," I say in a small voice.

And then she's laughing. She's laughing so hard, I'm afraid she's going to set off the monitors she's hooked up to. I have no idea what's so funny, but it is wonderful to realize her face, even so cut up, can still break out into such a big smile. It makes me believe she'll be okay way more than her assurance earlier about making the play.

"You're so right. I did buy a bullet journal as soon as I got your video reply. And around New Year's I bought this weird supplement my aunt suggested at Christmas that's supposed to give you more focus. And when someone in my AP chem class told me she felt ten times more rested after ten minutes of yoga, I managed to fit in some child's poses between chorus and chess club. Because I was super willing to take anyone's advice as long as it didn't get in the way of the super-destructive thing *I wanted* to keep doing. I wasn't ready to listen to anyone who was actually calling me out. So I guess, if you want to feel like you're a part of this, you're one of, like, seven enablers. But this isn't on you any more than the girl in AP chem. It's on me."

I sit down on the chair by the door, hard, hoping Jessica doesn't notice the shuddering breaths I'm trying to suck down as subtly as possible, because I believe her, and the guilt that had been previously flattening my lungs and other various essential organs has lifted, and it's apparently necessary I make up for lost time, breathing-wise.

"You okay? I know I'm technically the patient, but you look way shakier than I feel."

"I'm fine," I say, in an overly confident but still out-of-breath wheeze.

"So . . . do you want to play Heads Up! or something? Tyler'll be here in two hours, but I'm so bored of listening to podcasts, and I'm still not allowed to look at screens for very long."

"Sure," I say, scooching the chair up closer to her bed with minimal scraping sounds and pulling out my phone so I can load up the game.

"So you're HeretoHelp. We probably should have figured that out sooner."

I put down my phone and stare at her. Did I have some kind of tell, too, even with the void filter? Did I use my hands too much or something?

"What do you mean?"

"You're always the one fixing our messes in drama. Like, you know that robot in *WALL-E* that just follows the dirty line, cleaning it up, endlessly? You're like that. Makes sense you'd want to kind of prevent or, I don't know, triage some of the messes. Of course, some of us are way too messy to be helped. By a sixty-second advice video, anyway."

I pick the phone back up and open the app, before flipping it to my head. She reads it then looks down, I guess to avoid any more screen time.

"Dead or alive? Are you going to tell everyone it's me? You can, if you want. Talley and Essie know now, so they might beat you to it," I say, registering that possibility for the first time. It doesn't seem as horrible as it might have a few minutes ago, though. Because if Jessica can forgive me, surely the rest of drama can, right?

"Dead. Nah. That's your big reveal. Plus, and I know you're not normally on this side of it, but this could potentially spark some drama-drama, and I don't want to be the one responsible for that. Especially this close to opening night."

"Actor or musician? You think people will be pissed?"

"Actor. You must have heard people talking about it, which means you kind of knew you had everybody listening, but no one knew it was you. People might feel weird about it. But they'll get over it."

"Comedic actor or serious actor? What percentage of people do you think will feel weird about it?"

"Comedic, but he did some sad stuff. And some really dark stuff that freaked people out, because when you expect an actor to be funny and you walk out of his movie sadder than you entered, it seems like a trick. And I'm not good at hypothetical math. But forty percent of drama will feel weird about it, maybe?"

"Is it Robin Williams?"

"Yup."

"And you're sure you're not a part of the forty percent?"

She smiles and motions for me to give her the phone, which she puts to her head, displaying the name of a person I have absolutely never heard of, meaning I'll have to break the name into bits and do charades.

"I think near-death experiences make you very forgiving. Or maybe I'm just super grateful for the advice. I'm really into bullet journaling now."

SEVENTEEN

I've never wanted to put off spending time with Sadie before. But I know as soon as I actually confront her about the abstinence bet, there's a chance it will go from a thing she possibly said to a thing she definitely said. And I'm not ready for that yet. After circling the block three times, I'm still not ready, but I am resolved. I walk to her front door and ring the bell.

"Hi, Mia. Sadie's in the solarium. Come on in," Sadie's mom says, opening the door for me. The first time she ever directed me to the solarium, I had to google it while I was taking off my shoes. It took me a few dinners over here to realize Sadie's mom, a poetry professor at the community college across town, isn't being pretentious, but just genuinely enjoys using lyrical words as much as possible. And she makes the absolute best corn bread. Surely you didn't invite someone over to meet your mother and eat her corn bread if they're just part of a (lack of) sex bet, right?

I can hear the music before I see her. Something classical and dramatic. Being around someone who plays classical music a lot, even if you absolutely love it when they play, doesn't automatically increase your knowledge of classical music, so I don't know the name of the song she's playing, but I do know she's playing it with her eyes closed, and not in a party trick "Look, Ma, I don't even have to look at the keys" sort of way, but in a dreamy-trance way, like she needs to close her eyes so she can understand the music more. She looks so in control behind the piano, like I could rip the keys out from under her and she'd just keep playing air keyboard, because if the music is in her fingers, does she really even need the instrument? I'm so completely in love with her, and I don't want to ask her questions that might confirm things I don't want to know, I just want to stand at the edge of the solarium and watch Sadie make music. But eventually she opens her eyes and sees me. She smiles without stopping, telling me with a look that she's happy to see me. Or maybe that's just what I want to see. Like those bad lip-reading videos. Yes, I might technically know that the ref isn't whispering about how much he wants the Filet-O-Fish, but when they make him say it, that's for sure what it looks like he's saying.

I walk over to the bench and sit next to her. It's a romantic tableau that has yet to get old. Me and my musician girlfriend, sitting on a tiny bench barely big enough for both of us, both completely content being so close.

"Do you have an abstinence bet with your brother?" I ask. Sometimes you need to be direct.

She tilts her head and smiles like she's trying not to laugh. At me?

"No, Mia, I do not have an abstinence bet with my brother."

She's looking at me like she's waiting for me to ask a follow-up question that will illuminate why I asked the first question. But I don't want to: I just want to take her simple denial as is. Because I want to believe her so badly. But I've watched enough true crime cult documentaries to know you can ignore some seriously dangerous stuff when you *want* to believe what seems increasingly unlikely. Especially when the dangerous stuff is connected to a person who tells you you're wonderful.

"Talley heard you at the concert. Telling one of your friends that you were dating 'some ace girl' to win the bet. So I know. But I guess that would have been months ago. So if you feel different now, you can just tell me and I think I'll be able to forgive you, and maybe the whole thing will just be this funny little blip in our story a year from now . . ."

I'm rambling, and I know it might be a little undignified to admit I'll forgive her before I've even gotten a full confession, let alone an apology, but I just know that I will.

"Mia," she says, grabbing my hands. "Do you really think this whole time, every time we've hung out, every text, every kiss, I was just using you?"

I'm crying now. I don't want to be, but I am, not even just dramatically glistening eyes but hot tears running down my checks in what I know must make me look splotchy and childish.

"I didn't think so. But Talley heard—"

"Talley heard words and apparently didn't quite make out the dripping sarcasm. My old friend from orchestra camp was giving me a hard time for dating someone after the whole expulsion thing, so I sarcastically told them I was dating you to avoid sex. And when Talley went off to mis-overhear more people, I assume, we laughed, and I continued to tell them how amazing you are and how happy I am. Because, and I will say it as many times as you need to hear it, we do not have to have sex for me to be happy with you. Do you believe me?"

I do believe her. Because that honestly makes more sense than a no-sex bet, but also because I believe her in general. I believe she cares about me, because she's always been there when I needed her. Even sometimes when I didn't even know I needed her until she was there, which seems like a kind of superpower you can only develop if you genuinely like someone.

This is good news. I should be happy now, with this news, which should mean I should stop crying. But a combination of extreme relief and pent-up emotions still not tackled from the screaming match with Talley and Essie and all the catharsis with Jessica makes me start to cry harder. I'm sobbing, and Sadie reaches out and then I'm sobbing on her shoulder, and she doesn't ask what's wrong or assure me that everything is going to be okay; she just holds me and rubs my back, and waits for me to be ready to talk. She isn't demanding anything from me—she's just letting me know she's there.

"I started an anonymous ReelLife channel to give people in drama advice since no one ever listens to my non-anonymous advice, and I knew, I knew I could help them if they'd just listen, and today Talley and Essie found out it's me and called me a manipulative puppet master and then we screamed at each other, and I'm pretty sure they hate me forever now. And I might hate them a little too."

This last part is news to me even as I say it, but I realize it's true. I didn't think it was possible to hate your friends, but maybe when you let your anger toward them grow for long enough, that's what it has to turn into. I hate that I already feel responsible for letting the hate even happen. That even after everything, I still feel responsible.

Sadie pulls back a little to look at me.

"Well, that's a lot more intriguing than a sex bet."

"Also I thought I might have almost killed Jessica, but it turns out that was mostly from a kind of overconfidence in my ability to fix everything, which I'm starting to see is just a different kind of narcissism."

"I'm pretty sure we all have different kinds of narcissism. It's nice that you're using yours to try to help people. But back to the ReelLife channel. What exactly were you puppet-mastering them to do? Rigging some kind of drama election or something? I thought you were already queen of the backstage people."

"I was just trying to convince them not to make decisions that actively harmed them. I just wanted them to be happy. I wanted everyone to be happy."

"That is an admirable but ultimately too lofty goal. But back to the accusations. Aren't there like a million anonymous advice accounts on that app that is sucking the time and soul from our entire generation—"

"Well, now I'm going to delete it."

"No, I say that knowing I spent two hours last night on the Music Mistakes Subreddit. Our last freedom of choice is what thing we let suck up our time. But the puppet mastering?"

"People in drama are not as good at making themselves anonymous as I am. Seriously, if they ever go on the news as a witness and appear as one of those shadow people with a voice changer, they would out themselves immediately. I almost always knew who it was, so I could figure out what they really needed to hear."

"Huh. Okay. Yeah, I can get how that could be a little shady."

"You think?" I ask. Sadie calling HeretoHelp a little shady stings way more than anything Talley and Essie said about it. And I hadn't even told her about being Jessica's seventh enabler.

"I don't think you *meant* to be manipulative or anything, but you knew they weren't getting what they were very confident they were getting—advice from a stranger. It sounds like at the very least you engaged in false advertising, and even celebrities selling vitamins can get fined for that. I can see people getting pissed."

The idea that people could be angry at me would have been a terrifying prospect even a few days ago. But it seemed slightly less so now, maybe because I knew for sure at least two people were, and at least two people weren't. And Sadie and Jess were right. I hadn't been totally honest, and I'd apologize for that. After the apology, if people were still angry, there was nothing I could do about that. I couldn't dictate other people's feelings. No matter how bad I wanted to.

"What should I do?" I ask.

"You want my advice?" Sadie says, with a slight smirk.

"Yes, irony, full circle, less amusement at my expense, more help, please," I say, smiling.

"Sorry. I think you should be good with a basic apology. Your advice helped most of the time, I assume?"

"You'd assume that?"

"Of course. You're very wise. And you know more about your drama people than Beliebers know about Justin Bieber."

"I don't think there are any Beliebers anymore."

"I do not have time to keep up with pop music—"

"Was there a name for Mozart fangirls?"

"You're stalling."

I nod. I am. I make a "please continue" hand gesture.

"Right. If you really helped most of them, then you should have enough goodwill to sidestep puppet-master accusations from most people. I've known you for way less time than your drama friends, and I know you're not a malicious mastermind. You're a very kind and caring mastermind. I'm sure if you confess now, all will be forgiven by the time the musical goes up."

"The blowup I just had with my two best friends might suggest forgiveness isn't that much of a given."

"Mia, I want to say some things to you about Talley and Essie, but I don't want to pile on if you're already too distraught. Could you rate your emotional turmoil on a scale from one to ten for me?"

"I don't think I'm ever aware enough of my emotional turmoil to give it a rating. But let's say since my heart and soul have already been crushed today, it seems unlikely they can get more crushed, you know?"

"That is incredibly shortsighted of you, but I'm going to run with it. Talley and Essie are not good friends."

"Talley and Essie are my best friends," I say, which is not really a counterpoint but just something I feel like I need to say. In case Sadie forgot. In case I forgot.

"Yes. No, I get that. And I'm not saying they're bad people. I'm not even saying you should cut them out of your life or anything, because people can grow and change and having history with people is powerful. I'm just stating a fact I think is really, really important for you to absorb. They have not been good friends to you. And you've been a really good friend to them."

"Except for the whole thing where I knew why Essie was really skipping prom and I knew Talley didn't get into any New York colleges and

I didn't tell them. From the app," I clarify, as I suddenly realize I hadn't explained the biggest reason Talley and Essie blew up at me.

"So that's maybe a slightly awkward situation, but no one was in danger, and they decided to not actually confide in you. But I have watched you drop everything when Essie needs to talk, and be Talley's personal music critic, while you just get dismissed. I don't even know if you register it, but I have seen Essie stop listening to you midsentence like a teenager in a comedy sketch about rude teens, only you're the mom. It's jarring. You have no idea how many times I wanted to scream, 'You're missing it—Mia's being funny, or sweet, and you're missing it.' Did you ever think that all your friends in drama who aren't taking your advice might just be following their lead? Like, if your best friends ignore your advice, why should anyone else take it?"

I hadn't thought of that. And I had spent a lot of time deliberately not thinking about the missed calls and texts left unanswered when I needed them, because they were busy. They had passions and goals and direction. And I was just me and would figure it out eventually. But maybe that wasn't the point. The fact that I would be okay didn't mean I didn't want someone there while I wasn't quite okay yet. To listen. To just be with me.

"Is it bad that I already miss them? I mean just the idea that this fight is going to keep us from talking, the idea of not talking makes me miss them? Does it mean there's something fundamentally wrong with me that I know you're right, and there's still this voice in my head saying, 'Fix it, fix it, fix it'?"

I put my head on Sadie's shoulder.

"Like I said, I don't think they're bad people. I think they could become good friends, if they wanted to. But you have to let them know that's what you need. That if you're going to keep this friendship up, you're not going to be waiting-in-the-wings girl."

"But that's where stage managers are supposed to wait," I say, smiling.

"So joking's okay now?"

"When I'm doing it," I say.

"Do you want to go get some dinner? I don't think you need to plan your apology right now."

"Absolutely. I can't think of a better way to avoid my problems for an hour or two."

"Maybe I'm a bad girlfriend, but I have no problem letting you hide with me," Sadie says, threading her fingers through mine.

"You're the best girlfriend," I insist.

"I bet you say that to all the girls."

"Because I want to move forward with complete honesty, I have told a lot of girls in drama they're the best girlfriend during various relationship pep talks, but I now realize I was wrong and it's you."

Sadie starts laughing, and then I'm laughing too, and it doesn't make me forget the deep ache in my chest, but it does let me know I have someone who cares the ache is there and isn't going anywhere as I try to make it hurt less.

———

I resist looking at my phone for all of dinner, only peeking when I'm back in my bedroom. From the complete lack of text messages, I assume Essie has left the task of revealing my secret identity to everyone in drama to me. Before I confess in the group chat, I decide to try out the big reveal on Brian. I know I technically had a dry run with Jessica, but being in a hospital room makes almost anything seem more dramatic. I know Brian has seen some of HeretoHelp's videos because he mentioned one at dinner last month, but I'm pretty sure I never gave any advice to his friends, so he shouldn't have any personal stake in it. Except for, of course, undying loyalty to his sister and all her endeavors (hopefully).

I knock on his door.

"I am not naked," he says, which I know means I can come in.

Brian is lying on the floor, arms above and pressed to either side of his head like he's about to dive into a pool, toes pointed.

"Whatcha doing?"

"I saw this thing on YouTube, that if you lie out and stretch for thirty minutes a day, you can grow up to an inch after a year."

"Brian, guys don't stop growing until they're like nineteen or twenty. You could grow more than an inch in a year just going about your normal life."

"Yeah, but this way, I'll know that I earned it. What's up?"

I move some of the empty soda cans off his bed and sit on the edge.

"What if I told you I had kind of a secret identity?"

Brian sits straight up.

"Is this a Batman thing or a gender-identity thing? Because I love you either way, but I'm going to be so excited if it's a Batman thing!"

"You think I have superpowers?"

"Batman doesn't actually have any superpowers. Just an unquenchable thirst for justice. And vengeance. And breaking stuff."

"It's not a Batman or a gender thing." I take a deep breath. I've been taking a lot of deep breaths lately. I wonder if they have the same beneficial effect they have in a yoga class if they're taken out of emotional necessity. "I'm HeretoHelp. You know, that advice ReelLife account?"

"Yeah, I know."

I stare at him.

"What do you mean, you know?"

"I told you, Chris showed me one of those videos. The one where you tell that girl she should drop AP bio right before the cat dissection or she'll never be able to look her cat in the eyes again. Then Chris and I spent basically the rest of the afternoon trying to get his cat to look us in the eye, but never could. I think Old Deuteronomy is hiding something."

"No, I know you saw the videos, but how did you know it was me?"

"Mia, we share a bedroom wall. I could hear you recording them. I just assumed you were sending your friends voice memos, but once Chris showed me the account, I got it."

"Oh. Right. Well, uh, I kind of want to get your opinion on it."

"The name could be a little catchier."

"Yeah, I know. That's not it. I could kind of figure out who everyone was even though they thought they were anonymous. So when I was giving them the advice, they thought they were getting advice from some random stranger, not a friend who knows stuff about them. Which Talley and Essie think is super manipulative and basically criminal."

"They didn't know it was you?"

"Well, not everyone in school shares a bedroom wall with me."

"Right, but, like, I would have known it was you even without that."

"How?"

"The shadow always grabbed the back of her neck whenever it came to a tough part of the question, like you do. And couldn't quite say 'undeniably,' like you can't. And used their whole hands to do air quotes like they're casting a spell, like you do. Just because I couldn't hear your voice or see your face in the video doesn't mean I can't tell when you're right there in front of me. I mean, isn't that how you figured out who your friends were on there? Who wouldn't recognize their friends?" He looks at me with genuine non-judgy confusion when he asks this.

And I realize he's right. I knew who Essie was because of her French phrase. I knew Talley because he was quoting me. It's not like anyone slid out of their filter or even revealed a particular telling corner of their bedroom wall or something. I knew them because I *knew* them. Because I paid attention to them. Because I was always paying attention and watching out and making sure everyone was comfortable and taken care of. I thought I *could* take care of everything and everyone so no one ever had to get hurt. After talking to Jessica, I was slowly realizing that was too much for one person to take on. And now, after talking to Brian and Sadie, it was becoming more and more clear that most of my friends weren't even trying to take care of me.

"But there is a 'reasonable expectation of privacy,'" he adds, stretching out on the floor again.

"What?"

"Like, the Fourth Amendment."

"No unlawful search or seizure," I say, that factoid bubbling up from sophomore year US government class before I remember I remembered it.

"Right."

"I didn't search or seize anything."

"No, I know. It's just, I think they might have had a reasonable expectation of anonymity. You got Addy to mess with the app to get more people in drama to see your videos, right?"

"How did you know that?"

"I remember when you went over there at the start of the school year. Put it together. I watched all of *Sherlock* last summer. I can put stuff together."

I nod. I'm not sure he has Sherlock-level deduction, but I have learned not to underestimate my brother.

"I think any time you have to enlist a hacker, and you're not doing something actively good, like breaking into a medicine factory to Robin Hood some medicine, you might be on morally shaky ground, you know?"

"Addy said it was okay."

I know this is not a good argument and makes me sound like a five-year-old, but I still cling to it. If my brilliant, kind, actual adult cousin thought it was fine, that must mean I hadn't done anything *really* wrong, right?

"When I went to Addy with my thing—"

"Which was . . ."

"Still a secret, she said she didn't like to pass judgment and was only going to stop us if she thought the plan was actually criminal."

"My plan wasn't criminal."

"Right. But I think you still have to apologize."

"I know. That's what Sadie said."

"Are you trying to collect more people who say you should apologize, or are you going to go through all your contacts until you find the one person who says you don't have to?"

Jessica's right. You only take the advice that lines up with what you're already willing to do. Luckily, I already know I have to do this.

"Just getting a second opinion. I know you guys are right."

"Don't worry. Even if all of drama turns on you, you can always hang out with the lacrosse team. After Rob put Nair in our shampoo freshman year, we only iced him out for, like, a week. We're a very forgiving group."

"I appreciate it, Bri," I say, getting up to leave. To start drafting my big apology. Or maybe I should think of it as my medium apology, so I don't get too stressed out over it. Plus, like Sadie said, there should be some goodwill there. I had helped them. Most of them.

"Hey, Mia?"

"Yeah?"

"I know sometimes I've gotten kind of distracted and maybe missed the exact details of your advice, but you know I always mean to follow it, right? Not to get mushy or anything, because I know you don't like mush, but I don't come to you for advice because of the whole right-next-door thing. I come to you because you're the smartest person I know. And someone who will care about solving my problem just as much as I do."

"I don't mind mush. That was very sweet mush."

"Go write the apology. If it goes badly, I'll be here."

On a day of heartbreaking revelations about who hasn't been there for me, it's extremely comforting to know I have a couple people who always will be. And they're pretty spectacular people.

EIGHTEEN

I always figured I'd do the confession thing as a video on HeretoHelp. It seemed like that would mean things had come full circle, that the senior prank—or social experiment or whatever it was in the end—was over, and, most importantly, releasing a video seemed like the most dramatic way to confess. But I knew now I didn't want to be dramatic. I wanted to be straightforward and clear. I wanted everyone in drama to know what I now knew—it was shitty that they didn't know I knew them. And even if I didn't mean to hurt them, being kept in the dark could very reasonably make them feel like I had violated an unspoken trust. I had to take responsibility for what actually happened, no matter what my intentions were.

I knew I couldn't fix everything, and maybe I should start thinking about why it was so important to me to try to fix everything. But there was also a part of me that was still just a little proud. I had come up with a way to get people to listen to me, and I knew, I knew Maria was better off without James, that Ricky was happier playing baseball, that I had proved

I could help people. I wasn't looking for a thank-you or anything. But I needed to acknowledge that for myself.

I had started composing the confession in my notes app with the intention of pasting it into the drama group chat when it was perfect. But an hour after first pulling it up, perfect seemed further and further away. It also occurred to me a quest for perfection is pretty close to a quest to create a conflict-free world (at least, the world directly around me), and that was an impulse I was trying to curb. My phone buzzed, and for a second I thrilled with the possibility it might be Talley or Essie ready to make up, or even Talley and Essie ready to berate me some more but still wanting to talk to me, but the screen lit up with Addy's name. I answered the FaceTime call.

"Tiniest cousin! How's life! General life things, nothing specific," Addy says. The phone is pointed at her ceiling, as it often is when she makes FaceTime calls. She feels no obligation to actually show her face, and most of the time she seems to call from her kitchen while she's chopping or blending things.

"Brian told you I'm dealing with the consequences of my senior prank?"

"Actually, he told me you were gearing up for even more consequences. Aren't you writing your confession? Are you going to do it as a dramatic monologue? Or, ooh, how about an interpretive dance."

"Addy, I know you went to a tech high school, but you must have figured out every performing arts kid isn't an extra in *Fame*."

"Not with that attitude you aren't. But Brian had a specific request. He wanted me to, hold on . . ." Now I can see her face hovering over the phone that's clearly still flat on a counter, her gummy-bear-shaped earrings swinging wildly as she tries to locate whatever my brother messaged her.

"Yes, here. He wanted me to 'be a not-quite-parental adult to guide you during this trying time.' I'm not completely sure what a not-quite-parental adult would do. Are you looking for some stern glares, or maybe I could tell you about how hard things were in my day to put your problems in perspective? 'We didn't have any of this ReelLife. When we wanted to send our friend a text, we had to see if we still had text credits left for the month like we were in a goddamn dystopian YA novel. And a new goddamn dystopian YA novel that we had to read and create new fan fiction around came out every week.' How's that?"

"Maybe I could send you the draft of my confession, and you can tell me if it sounds okay?"

"I could do that. But my notes would include where you could add just a little bit of dance. It's important to play to your audience."

I text her the note and try not to watch as her eyes dart back and forth as she reads it.

"This is pretty long."

"Too long?"

"Well, the average human attention span has been steadily declining over the last few decades. And I think that goes double for you youths."

"What should I cut?"

"Most of it?"

I put my phone down face-first on my bed so Addy won't see me trying to smother myself with a pillow.

"Miiiaaaa" I hear her call, the mic muffled a little in my blankets. I pick the phone back up and blink at her.

"I'll just let Essie tell on me. Everyone gets the same information, and that way the format of the confession is one thing I can't possibly be blamed for."

"I think if someone else is explaining your misdeed, it technically becomes an accusation, not a confession."

"I don't think you're being very not quite parental," I grumble.

"Sorry. I should have been more specific about cutting everything. I just mean I think you should keep things simple. I mean, you don't just want this to be a confession—you want this to be an apology, right?"

"Right."

"Well, the more you start explaining things in an apology, the closer you get to just listing excuses instead of actually expressing remorse. The only thing worse than never apologizing is doing a non-apology, you know?"

"I know."

"If I'm getting you to say 'I know' in a defeated yet sort of whiny way, I think I might be getting a little too close to parental."

"What's the worst thing your best friend ever did to you?" I ask, suddenly. I know it might seem like I'm trying to change the subject from the confession draft, but really I just know Addy's right, that I need to keep it short and simple, and now I'm ready to get some wisdom on another swiftly crumbling piece of my life.

"You and Essie and Talley in a fight?"

"Yes. It might be more than a fight. Possibly a war? I don't know. I've been so good at avoiding conflict for the last eighteen years, I don't know that I'm good at identifying different kinds of them. What's the difference between a fight and a war?"

"I could text my friend Jason, who works at the Pentagon, and ask, but I think a war involves a declaration. Have any of you guys declared anything?"

"Well, according to this online dictionary, to declare means 'to make known or state clearly,' and since I have no idea where we stand and would love some clarity, I guess not."

"Well, that's good, I guess. To answer your other question, no horrible misdeed perpetrated by a supposed friend comes to mind."

"It would be a lot more helpful to me if you'd had a slightly more traumatic adolescence, Addy."

"I'm sorry. I was spending most of my prime drama years learning Python. But last summer when I broke my ankle, I watched all of *Dawson's Creek* in a week and a half. And they went through some stuff. I could give you some episode recaps, if you think that would help."

"I also have access to Wikipedia. So I'm good. But did the good people of *Dawson's Creek* happen to have an arc about when it might be time to stop being friends, completely?"

"That bad?"

"The fight? Yes. No amount of squishing Mom's old stress ball is getting exactly how angry they looked out of my head. But I've also started to realize that even before the yelling, they might not have been the *best* best friends."

"Well, yes, but I thought you knew that?"

"Okay, I'm going to need you, everybody, if you have important information about my life you think I already know, to run it by me, just in case. Why would I continue being friends with people who weren't good friends if I recognized that? And how did you know they weren't good friends?"

"I mean, why does anyone stay in a relationship that's not as amazing as it should be? Fear of change, comfort of familiarity, the inside joke that every once and a while simultaneously reminds you of the good times while convincing you that you have some kind of magical link to this person who just *gets* you. And I've known they were bad friends since they didn't come to visit you after you got your appendix out when you were a freshman."

I hadn't thought about that in a long time. I had been so terrified I would never wake up, and my death would leave Mom and Dad so devastated that Brian would feel like he had to watch over them, which would mean he could never leave home, so because I didn't invest more in appendix care (I had an even shakier grasp of anatomy when I was fourteen than I do now), I was sure I was going to ruin the lives of three people I loved with my stupid death.

"It was the week before the spring show and the spring concert," I say. "They were busy."

"Yeah, they were also fourteen. Absolutely nothing catastrophic would happen if they took a few hours to spend with their supposed best friend who was in the hospital. Actually, I take back putting an age on that. Anyone should be able to find the time to visit their friend in the hospital."

"I wasn't mad at them. I understood."

"That was how I knew they weren't good friends. The fact that you weren't mad at them could just be your generally forgiving nature. But the fact that you understood, like you didn't even register that it should hurt? That meant they already hadn't been there for you a lot. They had somehow set up that expectation for you."

I had always thought being understanding was just something good I had within me. Like compassion or a vast knowledge of the cutest types of frogs—a combination of traits and things I'd cultivated that I was lucky to have. But it's seemingly increasingly possible the understanding is less a virtue and more a coping mechanism to deal with two people who I've had to extend more understanding toward than I probably should have.

"Sadie thinks I should give them another chance. That maybe we can make up and use the making up as a time to talk about a future where they're better friends. And I'm a better friend, too. I did keep secrets from them."

"That could happen."

"But do you think I should try to make it work? Or just use graduation as a natural way to kind of, I don't know, float away?"

The idea is horrifying even as I say it. I try to picture a future where Essie isn't texting me after an audition or Talley isn't sending me his latest song, or we're not all on some weird combination of video chats to virtually crowd around and judge a new viral video. That future sounds terrible. But I also don't know if doing those things would be the same now that I can see so clearly how the space around those moments has been filled with other moments when I needed them and they weren't there.

"Mia, I can't tell you what you should do," Addy says, gently. "I really can't. I can tell you I would probably cut ties and hope for better friends at college, but I also know us computer people are cold and detached, so you probably shouldn't be listening to me."

As if on cue and unaware of her sarcasm, Addy's elderly guinea pig, Frank, scurries up her arm and starts nuzzling her cheek. She pats him on his tiny head and looks directly into the camera, waiting for me to say something.

"I want to try." And I really do. Not because I'm afraid to start from scratch breaking in new best friends, or because so close to the end of high school I'm getting nostalgic. I know I love Talley and Essie, no matter how angry I am with them. But I also like them. They're funny and introduce me to new shows and snacks I never would have found otherwise, and there have been moments, many moments over the course of our friendship, when I looked at them both and felt like together, we were something special. "I'm not ready to give up on, what did you say? Our magical familiarity yet."

"Well, then, you have a busy weekend ahead of you: things to confess, whole relationship dynamics to destroy and rebuild. Remember to take screen breaks for your eyes and to hydrate. It's very important to hydrate."

"I don't know where I'd be without your words of wisdom, Addy."

"Hey, that's an idea. Do you think I should start a ReelLife account giving advice?"

"Goodbye, Addy."

"It wouldn't be anonymous, because I'd want all the glory. But not everyone is lucky enough to have an older cousin looking out for them. I could be helping so many more of you guys."

"Do you want me to text you an update with how it all goes?"

"Of course. And I'm here to talk if you need to. However it goes."

"I know. Love you."

"Love you too."

I hang up the phone and stare at my screen saver. It's a picture of Talley and Essie and me in eighth grade. It always felt like such an accomplishment, being a part of a core group of friends. It might be time to consider what accomplishments I have without it.

I put my phone on the book stand. I never did get around to buying an actual professional phone stand. Maybe because that would make the whole thing more real, not a senior prank but something that was actually important to me. I spend just a few minutes fixing my hair and making sure I don't have anything in my teeth or any stains on my shirt, a new routine I never had to do when any imperfection would be obscured by the void. I take a deep breath and hit record.

"Hey, everyone. HeretoHelp here. Though a lot of you know me as Mia. And I need to confess, I know a lot of you too."

NINETEEN

After I post the video, I text Sadie asking her to come over and immediately put my phone under my mattress. I can hear it buzzing with notifications at a rate it's never buzzed before, and I'm about to google "can the friction of a buzzing phone against a mattress cause a devastating house fire" (from my laptop) when Brian appears in the doorway.

"You did it," he says.

"I did. Did you hear me stop recording or . . ."

"I got some texts."

I wait for him to expand on that, to say something like "I got some texts from friends who were like 'saw your sister's video, totally not a big deal'" or "I got some texts from drama kids to tell me to tell you that they're never speaking to you again." But he just continues to lean against the doorframe.

"Texts that said . . ."

"That you posted the video."

"Just the information relayed, absolutely no editorializing?"

"People were surprised."

"Surprised and angry?"

"It's really hard to tell what people are feeling over text."

"And sometimes in real life too. For instance, I have no idea if the texts you received have made you feel hopeful for the future of my social life or fearful for my future."

"I'm always fearful for your future; you're the one who explained what's going to happen to our water supply by the time we're Mom and Dad's age."

"I appreciate you trying to distract me with climate anxiety."

"Is it working?"

"It is not."

I hear footsteps coming up the stairs, and then Sadie is leaning on the other side of the doorframe. The two of them look like they could be the title image for a new Disney Channel show about two high schoolers who start their own restaurant coolly and confidently, while their girlfriend-slash-sister pops in to mix up the green peas and chickpeas for occasional comic relief. (I only did that once in real life.)

"Sadie, how are you possibly here this quick? I texted you like five minutes ago."

"Oh, I started biking over as soon as you posted the video. I was just giving you processing time, hanging out in the park until you texted."

I walk over to her with the intention of giving her a hug, but instead just kind of flop onto her body like one of those blow-up Christmas lawn decorations suddenly deflated.

"So, how are you doing?" she sort of singsongs.

"Brian won't tell me if people are mad."

"I think if people are mad, they'll send that information right to you."

"I'm too afraid to look at my phone."

"Do you want me to look at it?"

"No."

"Do you want to stand here in limbo until the fear of what might be rips you into tiny pieces?"

"Yes."

"Okay, well, you're not doing that. Where's your phone?" she asks, unhooking my arms from her shoulders and going into my room to search.

"I thought you were giving me processing time."

"Processing time is healthy. Letting the worry eat away at you is not. Shh, I think I hear it," she says, homing in on the buzzing and pulling the phone out from under my mattress. She's really very strong. I wonder if that is a product of piano playing, like her upper-arm muscles are pressured to keep up with her wrist muscles. I'm suddenly trying to think of all the situations where she might need to carry me, an inherently romantic act for a significant other to do: we have to cross a stream and I'm wearing fancy shoes and she's wearing rain boots. I've twisted my ankle. I have so many bug bites surrounding my ankle, I've convinced myself the structural integrity of said ankle might be compromised. I shake myself out of the daydream and watch Sadie as she looks at my phone screen for a second with an infuriatingly blank expression.

"What?"

"I've just never seen so many notifications before. I think this must be what influencers' phones look like all the time."

"Don't read the messages. Or even what they're from."

"I'm not reading them. I'm giving the phone to you, so you can read them. And whatever they say, I'm still here. And I love you."

I look up to see Brian attempting to casually exit. He waves and makes suggestive eye wiggles at me before he goes. I stare at Sadie. She loves me? I had hoped that she did, but asking outright was out of the question. Plus, I know some people might have a difficult time actually saying it out loud, and just want to express it through actions, like writing songs about you. But she really said it.

"Are you just saying that to try to distract me?"

"Mia, I know you're going through it, but that's the second time today you've accused me of being an actual monster, and eventually I'm going to have to start reading into that."

"You love me? Are you sure?"

Sadie laughs, with her eyes closed. It's my favorite laugh of hers, like she can't possibly take in any more delight from the world at that moment. I want to fill her with that kind of delight all the time.

"I'm sure. I've been sure for a bit, actually. Just wanted to keep you in suspense."

"I didn't want to say it first. I didn't want to seem needy. Or make things more serious, if you didn't want them to be," I say in a rush.

"I'm okay with things being serious. We are about to be high school graduates, after all. Time to be serious. Eat fiber. Be in committed relationships." She sits down next to me, our backs pressed against the bed, and grabs my hand. It reminds me of Halloween, leaning against the garage, looking outward next to each other, comfortable in being this close, so tangibly, obviously together.

"You know, I'm not worried about seeming needy," she says.

"I know."

"So, if you wanted to say something back . . ."

"Oh my god, shit, I love you too!" I say, horrified that in my complete and total happiness, I had forgotten to give her that key part of information.

"You drama people, always quoting Shakespeare," she says. I look at her, a little nervously, to see if I can tell if she thinks the fact that I forgot to say it back means I'm horribly self-centered, but she just looks happy.

"We could kiss now?" I ask. It seems like the proper romantic gesture for the moment. You seal things with a kiss, and this seems like a moment I'd like to be sealed, to keep it safe forever.

"I'd rather just hold hands, if that's all right with you."

"Really?"

She turns to look at me then. Still smiling, but a little gentler.

"Mia, I did not start dating you because of a sex bet. But what I told you this fall was maybe a bigger truth than I tried to play it off as. I did want to take a break from hooking up. Not because I had internalized slut shaming or anything like that. Just because I wanted to see what it was like, to get so close to someone without sex. Without making out, basically. Plus, I could tell you aren't that into it."

"I don't mind it, honestly," I say, but she puts a hand gently on my leg. It's such a nice way to be told, respectfully, to shut the hell up for a minute.

"I know you don't mind. If I thought you minded, I would have insisted on no kissing at all. But I'm not really into it unless the person I'm kissing is really, really into it. That's part of it for me, you know?"

"I could get more into it," I insist, but her hand is on my knee again, and I press my lips together tightly and nod.

"Maybe you will. If you really and truly feel like exploring, I will be happy to revisit making out. This whole year I've been thinking, I'll just follow Mia's lead. She's the one figuring this stuff out. I've got it figured out. I know my type and what I like to do, and my figuring out what I want a relationship to look like is done. And now I'm going to be completely and totally honest, but you have to promise you won't stress and freak out before I finish."

"I cannot promise that, but I will try to keep the freaking out to myself. I've actually gotten really good at that."

"You aren't as good at that as you think."

"Oh. Well. I'll try harder as I take in whatever you're going to say."

"I guess that's all I can ask. At the beginning, even at the beginning, I knew I liked you enough that even if I wanted something more, doing more than you were comfortable with, not doing that, not having that physical part of a relationship, would just be, like, the kind of less-than-ideal details that everyone in the world has with someone they're dating. Or is even friends with! They're wonderful and smart and funny and fun, so what if they have terrible taste in music or talk along with lines in movies you're watching for the first time—in the scheme of the whole person, it's a not a big deal. I thought that would just be your con column, you know?"

"I don't think I can handle hearing the rest of my con column now, but maybe later you could tell me so I could work on it," I whisper.

"It's not supposed to be a list you give someone to spark self-improvement or something, Mia, it's just a healthy way of looking at someone you love and knowing you don't have to love every part of them, or even every single thing you do together, to love them. But that's not even why I'm telling you all of this. I thought it was going to be this task, to

197

not have as much as a physical or sexual relationship or whatever with you. But I can tell you, in all honesty, in this moment, I'm just as happy holding hands with you as I would be with your hand up my shirt. Because this is how *we're* together. This is how *we're* a couple. And I love being us."

Sighing a lovestruck sigh out loud could be embarrassingly overdramatic, which might be in the same category as audibly freaking out, so I hold it in. But I want to. She loves being us. I love being us too. I love knowing that after a long day of rehearsing, all she wants to do is lie flat on the floor with our shoulders touching and listen to this podcast where they chronicle the seriously seedy lives of old famous composers, and I love that she's baked me "focus bars," which I'm pretty sure are just chocolate chip cookies squished into rectangles, every time I've had a big trig test. When I think about what "us" means, I picture the two of us leaning on each other, and I think when something is both completely literal and metaphorical that must mean it's important.

"So, not that it was my primary motivation for sharing all that, but did I distract you from what's waiting for you on the phone?"

"Yes."

"Good. I think that was enough of a mental break. Time to read."

"Right now?"

"Right now."

"And if reading them tells me every single one of my friends now absolutely hates me?"

"Then you can share some of mine. They're a little nerdy, and they will definitely judge you for not saying Bach the exact right way, but they're good people."

I take a deep breath, and scooch down away from Sadie toward the end of the bed. This is something I have to do with a kind of semblance of self-sufficiency. I look back at her and nod a little, and she takes out her earbuds and puts them in to show she gets that for a little while we're going to be doing what the child development side of ReelLife has told me is parallel play.

I ignore the ReelLife notifications and instead go right to my texts. I let my eyes go slightly unfocused so I can't quite see the names attached to the messages and instead count the blue dots that let me know someone has sent me one. Ten texts, one being the group chat where god knows how many individual messages have been added to the thread. I focus and open the most recent one, from Kylie, a sophomore techie I advised to ask her crush out. Since the crush was, unusually, not in drama, I had no idea if that one had actually worked out.

> I don't know if we're supposed to be mad at you or anything, but I'd never be with Mark if HeretoHelp hadn't told me to just go for it and ask him out. See you at rehearsal tomorrow.

She's capped off the text with a GIF of a dolphin animated to give a thumbs-up, a thumb badly digitally grafted onto the poor thing's flipper. It's creepy as hell and it's perfect. One person not mad at me. One person who will see me in rehearsal tomorrow and go about our business like nothing, or at least nothing bad, has happened. It is enough to greatly loosen the knot of panic firmly lodged in my chest. I open the next one, from Maria.

I'm not going to say it wasn't a little weird and maybe creepy that you knew it was us. But if that was the push I needed to end things with James, I'm glad you did it. I still trust you, just so you know.

I can feel tears hot and sharp in my eyes, but I blink them away. Crying makes reading harder, and I want to get through these as quickly as possible. I need to get through them, so it will be over, and I'll know exactly what damage has been done, so I can start to fix it.

Of the seven remaining non-group-chat texts, two are from people I gave advice to who express unconflicted gratitude; three are from people who I didn't give advice to who assure me it was a pretty good senior prank and praise me on my cloaking skills; one is from someone I gave advice to who says they think it was pretty manipulative; and one is from a freshman I can't even place who's apparently in the pit band and who thinks I need to give an in-person apology because, as she wrote, "doing anything that obscures the truth, even through a kind of lie omission, can pile on to the overall feeling that nothing can be trusted in this world, which will ultimately be one more thing that adds to our feelings of being increasingly unmoored." It's a humbling idea as well as really fucking eloquent, and I decide not just to take her advice, but find her to thank her for the idea in person as well. I'm still going through the group text responses, which seem to be an even mix of "totally not a big deal" and "kind of shady," when a text from Essie pops up.

You seem to be absolved.

By most people.

Talley's not returning my calls.

I don't know the kind of response she's expecting from me. Sympathy? Advice? A promise that even after our blowout, I would return her calls? The fact that I texted her back without a second's hesitation means I'm not exactly giving her the silent treatment, but I think my response was mostly out of habit. Or maybe curiosity? Or the hope that texting would naturally give way to talking, which would eventually lead to the complete repair of not just our entire friendship, but our entire history? Sometimes you can't wait for things to naturally fall into place though; you have to be the one to start them.

Do you want to talk? In person? With me?

You can come over here.

Why don't you come over here? Are you free in half an hour?

Maybe it's small and petty, but it seems important, in this moment, that the conversation happens at my house, at a time I select. I don't mean it to be a power play or anything like that. Just an assertion, a true one, that even though this is a big important conversation for me, it's not the only thing I have going on in my life. Actually, it won't even be the only big important conversation I have today.

Sure. I'll see you in 30.

I'm about to put my phone down and explain everything I've read to Sadie when I see the text dots oscillating again.

Are you going to ask Talley to come too?

It's tempting. To have everything all out in one conversation. To see if they can't repair what's broken between the two of them while we try to fix what's broken between the three of us. But it's become really clear that at least some of the problems with my friendship with Talley and Essie are grammatical. That I'd say "friendship" to describe two different friendships I have with two separate people. Two friendships I'd like to try to repair and continue whether or not they're able to stay together as a couple.

I think we should talk alone first.

I stare at the phone for a second. There's still this impulse to comfort her, to fix things for her. And I don't think that impulse is wrong. I might want to change our dynamic, but deep down, I don't really want to change me. I want to help people. Even the people who hurt me.

But if he texts, I'll tell him he should call you, when he's ready. He's not going to ignore you forever.

I have no way of knowing he won't ignore her forever. But it still feels good to comfort her. To let her know that that's something I still want to do.

TWENTY

Sadie rode home after I shared the texts and explained Essie was coming over. She offered to stay for moral support, but also pointed out that Essie's general disdain for her might make an already stressful situation even more stressful. We made a date tonight to watch a movie musical (she wants modern, I want classic, so we'll probably end up watching both), so at least I have a nice thing to look forward to even if my talk with Essie goes horribly wrong. I consider making some kind of list or speech or PowerPoint to prepare for our conversation, but in the end I spend the fifteen or so minutes waiting by scrolling through ReelLife, purposefully avoiding my main feed and hopping around to various cute animal accounts. I honestly am a little conflicted about whether you should put tiny animals into tiny outfits since it can be impossible to know for sure if they're enjoying it or not, but birds in miniature top hats are just so cute.

I hear the door open and footfalls on the stairs. We moved past doorbell ringing at each other's houses years ago, and it makes me feel hopeful that today's fight didn't make her feel like she had to revert to any sense of formality.

When she appears in the doorway, she doesn't pause to lean on the frame like Sadie and Brian, and instead walks into my room and gracefully sinks down to the floor to sit beside me. We sit in silence for a few not entirely uncomfortable minutes. I had decided that I would let her speak first. Just to attempt to gauge what she thought this conversation was going to be. Or maybe I just didn't want to risk saying the wrong first thing.

"Talley shouldn't have told you about Sadie's bet like that. He was hurt, but that doesn't mean he should have been a dick."

I nod. I'm not surely exactly what to make of the form, not the content. It's an apology, but on behalf of someone else, not her. A hopeful beginning maybe.

"I talked to Sadie. She was joking with her friend. I'm not starring in a remake of *She's All That*. We're in love. Officially. Or I guess there was no legal documents or anything, but we talked about it."

It sounds corny to say, maybe even unnatural, to say it as a state of being, but also thrilling. I've always been annoyed that romantic love seems to be held on this higher pedestal than any other type of love, and it's not like having someone in love with me is better than having someone love me as a friend or daughter or sister. But it is different, and thrilling in its differentness.

"Oh. Well, I'm glad she isn't actually awful."

"You thought she was, though, and didn't think it was important to share that with me?"

"You didn't tell me you were running an advice account on ReelLife."

"You didn't tell me about getting the *Spring Awakening* part."

"You didn't tell me about Talley's college rejections."

We sit in silence again. It sounds like a lot, batting the accusations back and forth all in a row like that. So many secrets and so much pain caused. And that's just from the last couple of months.

"You were happy," Essie says, finally. "I didn't want to be the one who wrecked that for you."

"Didn't you?" I say, the question coming out before I really have a chance to think about it. "You've spent the last seven months making it very clear you don't like Sadie and would prefer it if she wasn't sitting at our table or wasn't on the other end of my phone. It seemed like you wanted us to break up. Why not speed things along?"

"That's . . ." Essie picks at a loose string coming off the edge of her sleeve. "That's true. About me saying shit about Sadie, I mean. It was weird, not bad weird, just different, you having a girlfriend. Having someone else you might want to hang out with on the weekend, someone pulling at your attention. It was different, and so many other things were already becoming different this year, and that made me nervous, and that came out in bursts of bitchiness. Which I should have tried harder to keep in. But underneath all of that, I really was happy for you. I could see how much you were smiling, grinning, every time you looked down at a text from her, every time she walked into a room. I was glad you had that."

It really shouldn't surprise me that my best friend was rooting for my happiness, but it does, a little. Or maybe just that she was thinking about me, separate from thoughts about us.

"You really, really kept that to yourself. That's more than just 'bursts of bitchiness.' I never felt you be happy for me about this, even for a minute. I should have. You're my best friend, and I should have been able to tell you were rooting for me."

"You're right. I'm sorry."

It's the simplest of things. An admission, an apology in its most basic form. But it's something.

"Why didn't you tell me about getting the part?" I ask.

I realize this is me lobbing two accusations at her at once, instead of letting her ask for clarification on one of hers. I never really enjoyed watching Brian's lacrosse games, but I appreciated that the team always took turns trying to score goals. Brian has tried to explain to me so many times that they aren't actually taking turns, but I could see them all running to the home team's side, then the away's side, repeat, repeat with my own eyes. I maybe should have let Essie have her turn first, but I didn't.

"I wanted to tell you. I wanted to ask your advice. But I thought you might tell Talley, and I knew he would convince me not to take it. And I really wanted to take it, Mia," she says, looking at me with her eyes big and wide and hopeful.

"Being onstage with real working actors, having a director who gives us actual notes—it's everything I dreamed it would be. I was so terrified that the whole thing might be a letdown and I'd have to figure out something else to do with my entire future, but I know now, this is it. This is what I'm going to do forever. No matter how hard it is. And some of the older actors have already shared some stories that make it seem really, really hard."

"I'm happy for you," I say, because it's the simple truth. I think it might be enough to rebuild a friendship on. Two people who truly want the other to be happy. I hope it is.

"It wasn't my secret to tell, Talley's college thing," I offer. "But I should have talked to him about talking to you. Once I knew you both needed help, I should have told you right away that I knew, so you'd have someone you could talk to. So that you'd *know* you had someone to talk to."

"We were probably due for a fight, right? After seven years of peace? How long was it between winters in *Game of Thrones*?"

"Longer than that, I'm pretty sure," I say. We're both smiling.

And I realize here, I could let it go. Let us make up, then making up with Talley would be easy, and this whole thing would just be a slight tag on the end of the story of my brief stint as an advice columnist. I remember hearing one of Mom's friends talk about how her kids appreciated her more, actually reached out with explicit gratitude once they were at college. It's possible with some state lines between us, Essie would realize that our friendship was unbalanced and work to balance it out. At the beginning of the school year, I think I might have left it at that. But you can't give literally hours of advice without thinking more critically about the advice you give yourself, and HeretoHelp wouldn't advise leaving the kind of friendship this could be up to chance. I'm finally ready to take that good advice.

"You should have visited me in the hospital, Essie," I say. It's both direct and oblique, I know, and her expression immediately clouds with confusion and alarm.

"When were you in the hospital?"

"Freshman year. Remember?"

"Oh. Of course I remember. It was our first spring musical crash week. Have you been mad about that for the last four years?"

"I wasn't even mad about it then. But I probably should have been. It's kind of the most glaring example of you and Talley not always being the best friends."

She doesn't say anything for a bit. I'm slightly worried she might start crying, which would be concerning both because I don't want to make her cry, and also because that would mean I'll end up trying to comfort her, which will derail the whole "please be a better friend" conversation.

"I'm sorry," she says, in a small voice. It's not a voice I associate with Essie, queen of belting, of projecting.

"I think I might have already known that," she continues. "On some level, or maybe just in specific moments, I could tell we weren't showing up for you when we should have, but then something would be going on in drama or with Talley, and I knew you'd always be there and . . . I'm sorry. I can do better."

She is promising to do better. Such a big step. I could let it go again. But I think of Sadie and Addy and Brian listening in, and what they'd want for me. Maybe that's what I need to do for a while, think about how the people I know love me want me to be treated, and then demand that. Kind of like self-respect training wheels. So I look at a still teary-eyed Essie and keep going.

"You knew, on some level, that you weren't there for me, and you were just going to continue to not be there for me until we had some kind of epic fight? What if things never imploded? You just would have treated me that way forever?"

Essie is quiet again. I don't try to prompt her to talk. I want her to really think about what I said. Maybe for the first time ever.

"I think I would have. And that makes me so angry at myself, and embarrassed, that I've taken you for granted."

She turns to look at me then, intently. Essie has been honing her insistent stare for years for acting purposes, but it doesn't seem like an act now.

"I am so sorry. I was a terrible friend. I know I can be better. Will you let me try?"

I nod. I don't think I can trust myself to try to respond with actual words.

"I love you, you know. Officially."

"I love you too."

She rests her head on my shoulder. It feels familiar. That's not all you need to make a friendship work, but it's still nice to have.

"What do you think is going to happen with me and Talley?" she asks.

"I feel like that's a question I should be asking you."

"He was so angry. I've never seen him that angry. I don't think I've seen him angry at all, actually. Kind of annoyed, mildly pissed, but he's never been really angry, you know?"

"I know."

"We can make long distance work, if he wants to."

"Do you want to?"

She's quiet for a while.

"I don't know."

"You don't know, or you just don't want to say?" I ask.

"No, seriously, I don't know. I think I've been so successfully avoiding the question, I forgot to even ask myself."

"So, ask yourself now," I suggest.

More silence.

"It's possible to be scared of change and scared of losing your soul-mate at the same time. Just because one type of fear is there doesn't mean the other one isn't there too," she says.

"Okay."

"He is my soulmate. In the least corny way."

"I don't think there's a non-corny kind of soulmate."

"I just mean we fit."

"There might be other people you could fit with, though."

"I guess. But that's always going to be true. And you don't say that to people on their wedding day."

"Unless you're the best man who has been secretly in love with his best friend since the fifth grade, and reminding him that there are always more potential partners out there in the world is your last-ditch attempt at getting him to open his eyes and see what's been in front of him this whole time."

"Hitting the third-tier streaming rom-coms again?"

"Yup."

Essie stands up and starts gathering her stuff, a much calmer version of my exit last night.

"Where are you going?"

"I'm going to Talley's. If he wants to ignore me, he'll have to do it while I'm drinking tea with his mother or hanging out with his sister."

"And you want to do that now?"

"Not knowing what he's thinking, if he's thinking it's already over, is going to make my head explode, or maybe my heart, or maybe both. And I can't die before opening night."

"Well, this went pretty well. So talking to Talley probably will too," I say, trying to sound more optimistic than I feel.

"Definitely possible."

She finishes grabbing her stuff and starts to walk toward the door.

"I got you both tickets to opening night. I still hadn't figured out exactly how or when I was going to tell you, but I knew I had to, because I want you both there. If you want to, I mean. I don't want to assume anything."

"Of course I want to. But thanks for asking. Good luck."

"Really, Mia, after four years backstage, you don't know you're supposed to say break—"

"Not with the show, Essie. With the talk."

"Oh. Right."

I know my mom would insist I should walk her to the front door, but it feels right to stay on the floor and watch her walk away. This is the place where we started to build a new friendship. It's a place I'd like to stay for a while.

TWENTY-ONE

What's nice about closing night of the spring musical is no one is going to ask you why you're crying because absolutely everyone is crying—the freshmen because their first year is suddenly over, the seniors because everything is suddenly over, the sophomores because they're about to be upperclassmen, the juniors because they can now see, for a moment, how close they are to everything being over. Of course there are also extra, more personalized reasons for crying scattered among us, from break-ups to line flubs. I've been bursting into fresh tears any time I lock eyes with Essie, who has been allowed to spend our final night backstage even though she abandoned us, because drama club is more than an official cast list. Also, Mr. L has been pretty distracted lately, and I'm pretty sure he might think Essie is still in the ensemble.

There's about a twenty-minute chunk between the set changes in the second act, so I've given my headset to Julia and stayed in the choir room with Essie. It's almost eerily quiet, even though we can still hear bursts of laughter and applause from the auditorium. The choir room floor is absolutely covered in playbills and fast-food wrappers and cardboard from brand-new base and blush that had to be bought about fifteen minutes before curtain because someone spilled an entire Big Gulp in one of our makeup tubs. If I wanted to be the most responsible stage manager, I could use this time to start cleaning up, but I think I'm entitled to a little bit of senior slacking. If it even counts as slacking when I am actually going to clean in about an hour. Maybe slacking can just be a state of mind.

"Is Sadie coming to the cast party?" Essie asks. She's been better, these last few weeks, at asking boring, neutral questions about Sadie. It's a start. An important start.

"Yup. I'm worried it won't live up to all the excitement of the Halloween party, though. No performance or anything. Is Talley coming?"

"I think so. I mean, it's his last cast party too, with all his pit friends. I don't think he'd miss it. But who knows how much he's willing to miss out on to be sure he has to spend exactly no time with me," she says, attempting and failing to smile.

Actually showing up at Talley's house did not get him to end his silent treatment, and after another solid day of texts unanswered and calls ignored, Essie stopped trying. She told me it was because she was respecting his need for space and an overall desire not to become an actual creepy stalker, but I'm pretty sure each message without an answer was its own individual tiny nick to her heart. You can only collect so many of those before you have to protect yourself from bleeding out.

"Did he text you again?" she asks.

"No. I told you I'd tell you if he did. You trust me, right?"

"Yes," she says, spinning her phone on her knee. "I'm just hoping maybe you got so busy and distracted that you just forgot to tell me."

I had sent Talley a long apology of my own, and he had sent an almost chillingly impersonal "thnx," no vowels and an X, which is so out of character, I would have called his mom to make sure he wasn't abducted if I hadn't seen him at school the next day. But since then, nothing.

"I don't even know if we're broken up, you know?" Essie says. "I mean we're not, because we haven't had that discussion, but if he doesn't talk to me before I have to go to school, I'm not starting college explaining, 'Yes, I have a boyfriend, but I don't know if he's coming for the weekend because we haven't actually spoken since May.' I don't want to be that girl."

"I don't even think that's a type of 'that girl.' He's going to talk to you before August."

"I just . . ." She puts her head in her lap and talks at the floor. "We both kept things from each other. We have basically perfectly balanced wrongs. You and I talked it out the same day, and we weren't even close to balanced. Should I even want to be with someone who can't actually talk things out? What happens when we're thirty and he spends the money we were saving to freeze then unfreeze my eggs to pay off his gambling debt? We're just not going to talk about it?"

"Stop reading the Am I the Asshole threads on Reddit. Though, out of curiosity, which one posted the story?"

"In a twist, his cousin, who feels conflicted because they asked her to actually carry the baby, but now she's not sure she should bring a child into a family so full of conflict."

"I hope my life is never interesting enough to make it to the top of a Reddit thread."

My phone buzzes with the alarm I set to put me backstage ten minutes before the final light cue. I stand up and shake out my arms and legs, then my whole body like I've seen Brian do before a game. I'm not exactly sure if it's supposed to loosen up your muscles or get blood to them or whatever, but it feels productive.

"You coming, Es?"

"No, I think I'm going to stay here."

"Really? This is your last chance to soak up some genuine high school theater."

"I can still hear some of it from here."

"You know no one in the pit will be able to see you from backstage. If you're worried about that."

"I know. I just want to be alone back here for a little bit. Go and stage manage. They'll be lost without you."

I smile and walk toward the door. Before I go through, I turn and look at Essie. She's sitting in the middle of the risers watching something on her phone, one hand scrolling again and again, the other hand in a chip bag. There isn't any time to cry over the fact that that was our last backstage conversation. There's just enough time to be slightly wistful, then turn around and start the last final curtain of my high school stage-managing career.

TWENTY-TWO

"Stop saying it's a sex thing! It's not a sex thing."

"Mia, my love, my sweet, I am totally on board to go to your drama orgy. You don't have to be ashamed."

"It's just a nice thing we like to do."

"Which is probably the title of at least forty videos on Pornhub right now."

"It's completely innocent."

"And the rules are . . ."

"You have to be touching at least three people at all times."

"That is the rules of only two things: acro yoga and orgies. If we're going to do acro yoga, just tell me so I know to stretch. And borrow my mom's socks with the sticky things on the bottom."

We're in Sadie's car heading to the house of fellow senior Rachel's grandma's house and, more importantly, her three-acre backyard. No one can remember exactly what started this particular tradition, not even people like me who were completely sober at the time, but at some point at the cast party freshman year, we all ended up lying out in the grass, watching fireflies, and there were already couples holding hands and friends with their legs draped over each other's and people not quite accidentally knocking their bare foot against their crush's bare foot, and somewhere along the way, we decided to connect everyone, the entirety of drama and the band kids in pit and anyone else who showed up to eat too many chips and celebrate a perfectly serviceable Sondheim interpretation, by having everyone touch, toe to leg, hand to hand, elbow to side, at least three people at all times. And yes, I knew that a lot of the motivation for many of my dramatic brethren was fueled by the raging teenage hormones they warned us about in seventh-grade health. But for some of us, and I'm pretty sure more than just me, our resident asexual, it was just as important to be stitched into a group of people who wanted to be stitched into something with you.

"So, has all been forgiven? No lingering resentment coming out onstage or anything? I mean I didn't notice anything from the audience, but I know there's always plenty of things the audience misses. Were any of Sweeney's beheadings really about you?"

"He didn't actually behead anyone. And I'm almost all forgiven. With one notable exception," I say, my eyes drifting to my phone, as if I was hoping that just thinking about Talley's silence would be enough to break it.

"Hey," she says, squeezing my knee, "it hasn't been that long. I've had friends ignore me for a whole semester and eventually start talking again. There's still hope."

"Jesus, what happened?"

"What, with the semester silence? Uh, with Callie, sophomore year,

I didn't vote for her for class president. I told her I was never going to support someone who wasn't running on increasing the vegetarian options in the cafeteria, so she shouldn't have been surprised. And Eric thought I was flirting with this girl he thought he was in love with, when I was actually just tutoring her in pre-calc, and that's a good example of why you should never start a vow of angry silence until you at least confirm the facts you're angry about—"

"Okay, you have to stop. You're going to kill me with secondhand conflict."

"Have you ever thought about immersion therapy for that? I saw a newscaster do it once who was afraid of sharks, and after a few hours in the tank with them, he was petting them like they were puppies. You could binge one of the politics shows where the people in the little boxes are just shouting over each other."

"No thank you. And I think you should be just a little afraid of sharks."

"Letting go of your fears will set you free."

"Or destroy your inhibitions to the point that you're bungee jumping off things without a bungee cord."

"I've got it. We create a joint ReelLife advice account and give conflicting advice, and they pick which one they like the best. Or, or! We let the commenters pick which one they like the best, and whichever one gets the most likes, that's what the person has to follow."

"Sadie, you are going to make an excellent reality TV producer after you retire from piano playing."

"Who says I can't do both simultaneously? I'll be the first person to get an Emmy as a producer *and* composer for best original music. Do you think you'll be able to handle listening to me compose only the most tension-filled pieces in our tiny studio apartment?"

I freeze. Sometimes it troubles me, how much proof I have that in moments of heightened emotion I don't have the instinct to flee or fight. I assume my proclivity for a third option means I will definitely die in any dangerous situation. But that's a reality to ponder on another day, because right now Sadie seems to be implying we have a future that stretches out long enough to involve an "our" apartment, and I don't even know what to do with all the excitement filling my chest.

"Our tiny studio apartment?"

"I know, I know, us concert pianists sometimes wear very fancy outfits, but don't be fooled. I'll probably be a starving artist for most of my twenties; just because I'm taking a gap year to perform doesn't mean I won't eventually get into crippling college debt. Well, I guess I wouldn't technically be a starving artist, because my parents will always mail me granola bars. You wouldn't mind having our mattress live under the piano, would you?"

"You want to try to stay together in the fall?"

"And all the seasons after that," she says, smiling. And all the seasons after that. I feel like I'm going to melt into a puddle of a person at her feet.

"I also want that," I say, knowing that trying to put together a more complicated sentence and then saying it out loud with my swooning brain would be futile.

"Cool. So, now that's settled. What are you going to do about HeretoHelp?"

"What do you mean? I already published the apology."

"Yeah, that's what you did about how you used it to kind of mess with all your friends. But what are you going to do with it now that you've taken off the void filter?"

"Nothing? Delete it, I guess, so I don't have a bunch of notifications every time I open the app? Or maybe delete the app altogether."

"You don't want to give advice anymore?"

It's a simple question. Maybe even an obvious question. But not one I had ever considered. HeretoHelp was a distraction and a social experiment and a way to get the people in drama to listen and a way to make sure every word I said wasn't just screaming into the void. So once everything came out, and then (almost) everything was repaired, it never occurred to me that it could have some kind of life after.

"I guess I could. I did start it—well, one of the reasons I started it—to help people."

"And you did, right?"

"I did. A lot of the time, I did."

"And did you like that? Helping people?"

I pause. It was hard to separate how I felt answering people's questions and offering my advice from everything that came after. But in the end, how I feel about giving advice is actually simple.

"I love helping people."

"Then I think you should keep doing it."

"Maybe I will."

We sit in silence for the rest of the ride over. It's such a relief to have someone it feels this nice to be quiet with. I'm not worried she's thinking I have nothing interesting to say. I'm not even trying to figure out what she might be thinking about. If she has something she wants to talk about, she will. We're just two people in love enjoying each other's company. And it's absolutely wonderful.

———————

"If I'm making contact with a lot more than three ants, does that count?" Sadie asks from her place lying next to me, hand in hand on the dry grass in Rachel's grandma's backyard.

"Nope. But that is part of the experience," Essie says from just below me. Sadie and I each have one socked foot on each of her shoulders, and every once in a while Essie will squeeze mine. I like to imagine that from a drone photo, it would look like we were standing on her shoulders, perfectly balanced.

"I've got you, Sadie. Here's an elbow," says Jason, a flutist from the pit I assume Sadie knows from some music corner of the world. She accepts his connection offer.

"Well, this is embarrassing. Sadie's found her three connections before us, the real theater people," Essie says, a teasing smile in her voice.

"I could help with that."

I look up, and there's Talley, hovering above us. Essie squeezes my foot so tightly, I'm a little worried she might crush all the bones.

Without waiting for us to say anything, he lies down next to Essie and me, but doesn't move to touch either of us. We're all on our backs, so it's a little weird to look at each other, but maybe for this moment, it makes sense that we don't really make full eye contact. No one says anything for a while; we just listen to the conversations happening all around us, the sound of some people watching videos on their phones, a lone cricket or two brave enough to keep chirping even though they're living through what must seem like an *Independence Day*–level invasion of their previously peaceful space.

"So you're talking to me now?" Essie finally says, breaking the silence a little more combatively than I would.

"I just needed a second," Talley says.

"Interesting definition of a second. Talley seconds now last fifteen and a half days. Remind me to never bake with you."

"You never bake at all."

"I might have taken it up in the last fifteen and a half days. Plenty of time to pick up new hobbies, new perspectives, new languages."

"You learned a new language?"

"Maybe. My life is now just a mystery to you. It could continue to be a mystery. Up to you."

I can hear Talley sigh deeply. I'm terrified for a moment that he might decide to skip this entire attempt at reconciliation and go lie down on another patch of grass, but he doesn't move.

"I didn't just get rejected from the city schools I told you I was applying to. I got turned down from three New York City conservatories too."

"You auditioned?" Essie asks, turning toward him while still keeping our feet on her shoulders. "You said you didn't want that kind of pressure for the next four years. You said you wanted the chance to explore other subjects, and that people at conservatories forget how to do anything else besides music, and you felt your people skills were tenuous as is."

"Yeah, well, I was lying. I was afraid I wasn't good enough to get in. A fear that was, apparently, completely founded, because I'm not. I'm just a guy who plays guitar sometimes pretending to be a musician."

"Hey, hi, so I know this is very much a personal heart-to-heart between you two or you three," Sadie starts. "And I've got no insight into those relationships. But New York City conservatories' admissions are absolute bloodbaths. I mean, you wouldn't decide you're not really a student just because you got rejected from the Ivy League, right? You're using a really, really bad ruler to decide what you are and aren't. Okay, I'm not here now."

"Thank you," I whisper in her ear.

"And you already knew that," Essie says. "Not that it's not helpful to have it cosigned by a literal prodigy—thanks for that, Sadie—but even if you were interested in going to a conservatory, why wouldn't you audition for one here? You'd definitely get into New Haven Conservatory. Or Greenwich Arts."

"Because . . ." Another heavy sigh, this time a little tremulous. "Because that wasn't the plan. We had it all set up by freshman year. We were going to school together, in New York City. By the time I realized I really wanted to go for music, it seemed too late to mess with the plan. And when I got rejected by all of them, instead of going full self-loathing, I saved a little loathing for you, for keeping me from trying out in-state—"

"I would have told you to audition wherever you want, we will figure it out—" Essie's sitting up now and whisper yelling.

"I know. I know. But getting angry at you was easier than actually talking to you. So when I found out you had abandoned me before we even graduated—"

"I didn't—"

"I know. I'm not saying that's actually what happened—I'm saying that's what it felt like. What it felt like was that I shut all these doors for

224

you, and you weren't willing to shut any for me. So that's why I was so angry. I guess a little about the not-telling-me thing. But mostly that."

"You were angry at me for making a decision about your future you absolutely didn't give me the opportunity to even weigh in on, let alone make."

"Yes."

"And you're ready to talk now because you realize that's completely ridiculous."

"Yes."

Now Essie is the one who is deep sighing.

"Can we really talk tomorrow? Because I could pull up the audition schedules and rules for every conservatory in the state and figure out the best strategy, and then I could pull up maps and plan out when we would be able to meet up and talk FaceTime check-ins vs. text check-ins and all that right now, or I can tell you I love you and logistics will never get in the way of that, though two weeks of silent treatment in the face of conflict might, and tonight we can just enjoy our last cast party?"

"That sounds like a good plan," Talley says, taking Essie's hand. I let out a little sigh of relief. It was honestly involuntary and not meant to draw attention to myself, but it makes Talley look up at me anyway. His face suddenly looks pained.

"Mia, I am so sorry. I'm sorry I screamed at you, and that I didn't text you back while I was figuring out my shit with Essie when I knew the day after the fight that I was just taking things out on you that had nothing to do with you. I actually think the anonymous advice thing was pretty impressive. Better senior prank than anyone has ever come up with in drama, and I'm honestly glad you convinced Ricky not to attempt any more jazz squares. Last year I was convinced the poor guy was going to step right off the stage and land in the pit, killing someone in the brass section. You were doing a public service, and I'm grateful."

"You should let this go, you should let this gooo," a voice in my head is singing. Or at least put it off until tomorrow, like Essie is doing. Essie is smart, and following her lead could also be smart, and the fireflies are blinking and I just want to lie here with my best friends and my girlfriend in wonderful peace and tranquility. Unfortunately, I now have a more assertive internal voice that drowns out the calls to smooth out all conflicts, no matter what it costs me. Some of it still sounds like Brian and Addy and Sadie speaking on my behalf. But it's beginning to sound like me too.

"I appreciate that, Talley. And I am sorry I didn't let you know I knew about the college things so I could offer more support. But putting off talking things out with me for two weeks because you needed the head-space for Essie is kind of part of a larger problem with the entirety of our friendship and—"

"I know, I know. I wasn't not reading Essie's texts, just not responding to them—"

"And now you're interrupting me while I try to express my frustrations that you're not listening," I say, pointedly. Not mad, but not resigned either. Kind of with no-nonsense teacher energy. Maybe I'd like to be a no-nonsense teacher someday. I feel like both my life experience not being listened to and my newfound ability to demand listening could come in handy in that profession.

No one says anything for a moment, and I realize they're all giving me space to talk. That the quiet is for me to fill.

"You've been taking me for granted," I say. "But I think you can fix that. Do you?"

"You should probably give him explicit permission to talk now," Sadie says after another moment of silence, squeezing my hand.

"Right. So ends my speech. Anyone who decides to answer now is definitely not interrupting."

"I know," Talley says. "I mean, I didn't actively wake up and say, 'I think I'll be a shitty friend to Mia today,' but I think I did always kind of know I could be better. I hate that you might not know how much you mean to me because I was so bad at showing it. And just because I know the showing and showing up and everything will be something that has to build over time, I never would have made half the music I made in the last four years if you weren't egging me on, and I'm pretty sure I wouldn't have made it through high school without you. I'd just be stuck in the back of sophomore English class, hoping Essie will come and visit me and my emotionally stunted self. I love you, Mia."

"I love you too, Talley. And you *are* a musician. Fuck those conservatories. They'll want you to be a guest lecturer when you're famous someday, and you'll get to send them a really biting rejection. Or possibly go and take their money. That might be a better form of revenge."

"I will go directly to you for all my revenge advice," he says, taking my other hand.

"Hey, guys, we all have our three points of connection now," I notice.

It would have been nice to sit in the connected silence for a moment, but the very same second someone from across the yard yells out, "Sing, my angel of music!" Which means it's time for our sing-along. The rules are quite simple. Whatever song title gets shouted out first is the one that's sung. We mostly stick to musical theater modern classics or stuff from the last couple of shows, though sometimes people will go rogue and yell out "Bohemian Rhapsody" or something.

I've never picked one. It goes against so many of my deeply ingrained fears—of being too loud, of annoying people, of saying the wrong thing. But tonight is my last high school cast party. And I'm holding hands (and feet) with three people I love, who I know love me. People listen to my advice, and I'm going to keep giving it. People listen to me, and I have to stop being afraid of being too loud. Maybe people will like loud me. Maybe they won't, but it won't matter, because I will. I take a deep breath, open my mouth, and get ready to tell my friends what we're going to sing to the fireflies.

ACKNOWLEDGMENTS

Thanks to Lily Kessinger for believing in this book, and to Clare Vaughn for every insight she gave that made it better.

Thanks to my agent, Laura Crockett, for always being patient with my many questions and offering great advice.

Thanks to my thesis advisors Tracy Brain, Joanna Nadin, C.J. Skuse, and Gerard Woodward for guiding me through writing this novel from first ideas to rewrites.

Thanks to Philip Pascuzzo and Corina Lupp for creating such a beautiful cover, and the copy editors for catching my many typos.

As always, thanks to my mother, for all her support and always reminding me I am an author.